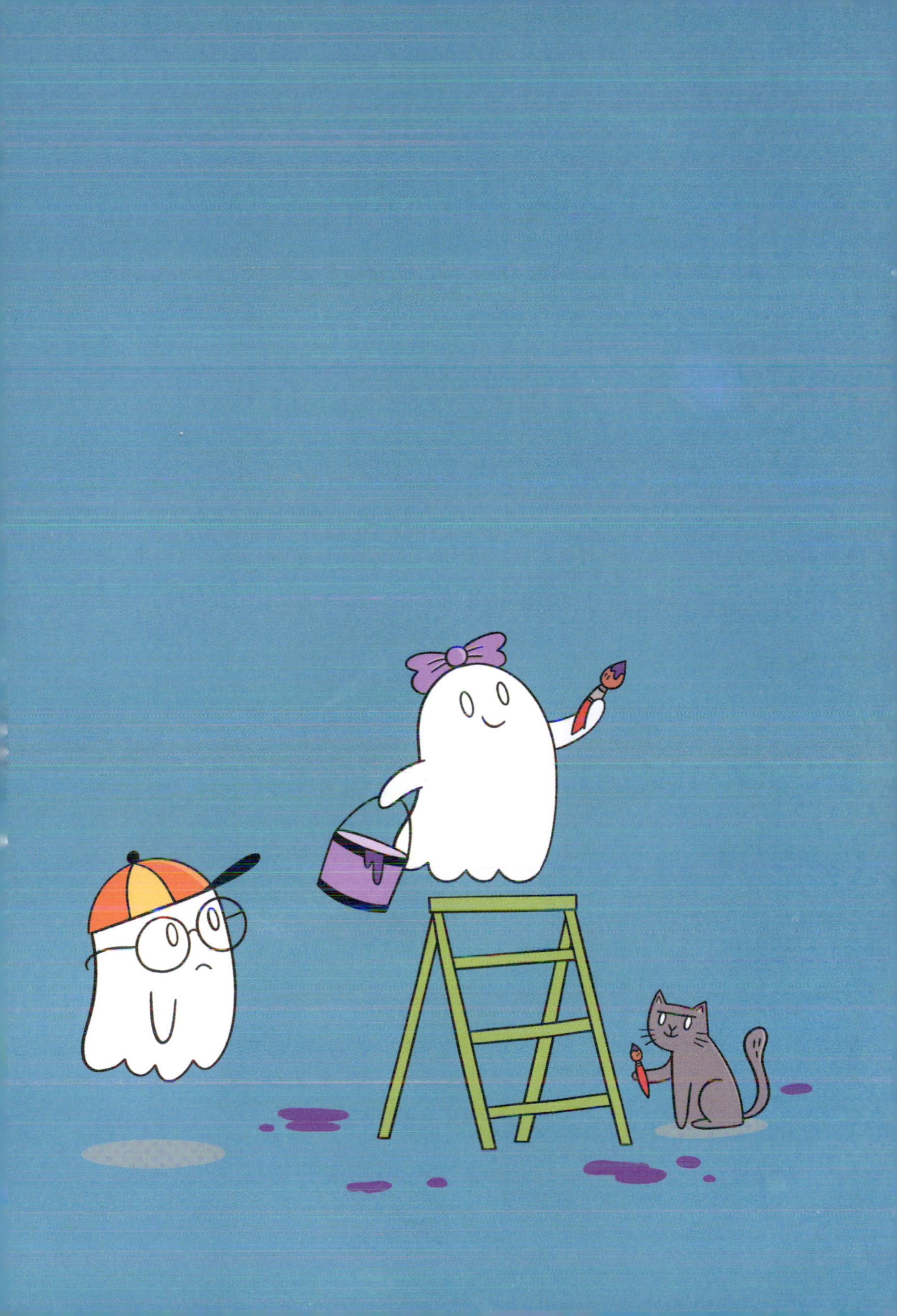

For Katie, my Cleo —H. F.

To the friends I made movies with:
Christian, Krista, James, and Jason —J. S.

Henry Holt and Company, *Publishers since 1866*
Henry Holt® is a registered trademark of Macmillan Publishing Group, LLC
120 Broadway, New York, NY 10271 • mackids.com

Our books may be purchased in bulk for promotional, educational, or
business use. Please contact your local bookseller or the Macmillan Corporate
and Premium Sales Department at (800) 221-7945 ext. 5442 or by email
at MacmillanSpecialMarkets@macmillan.com.

Library of Congress Cataloging-in-Publication Data is available.

First edition, 2022 / Designed by Sharismar Rodriguez and Mike Burroughs
Printed in China by Toppan Leefung Printing Ltd.,
Dongguan City, Guangdong Province.

ISBN 978-1-250-23945-7

1 3 5 7 9 10 8 6 4 2

A Fitz and Cleo Book

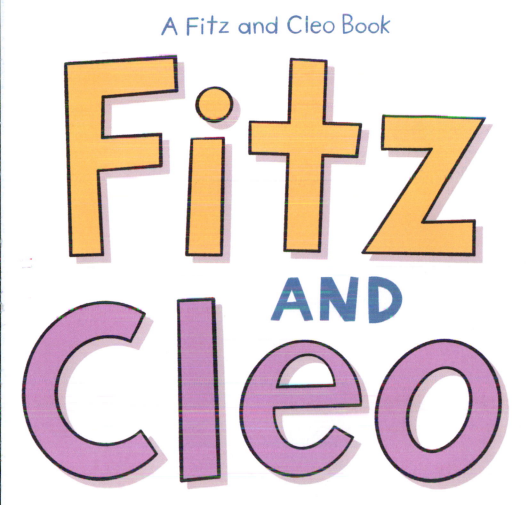

Fitz AND Cleo

Get Creative

Jonathan Stutzman & Heather Fox

Henry Holt and Company

New York

Head in the Clouds

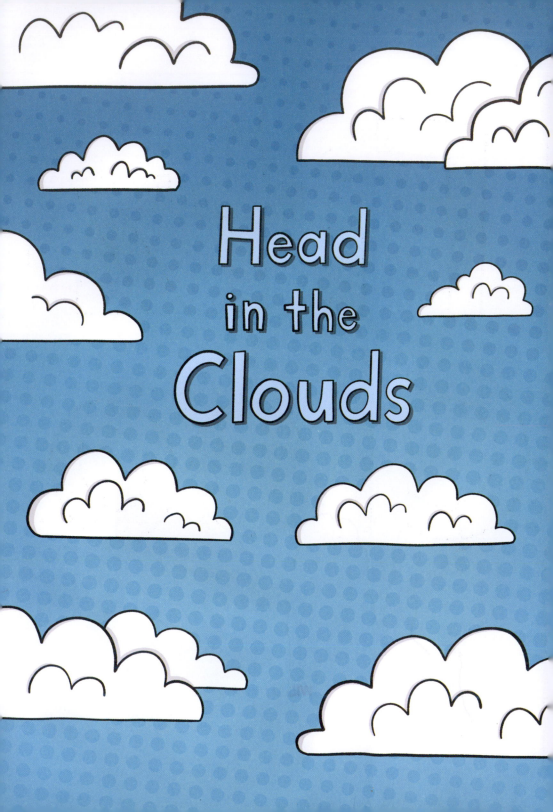

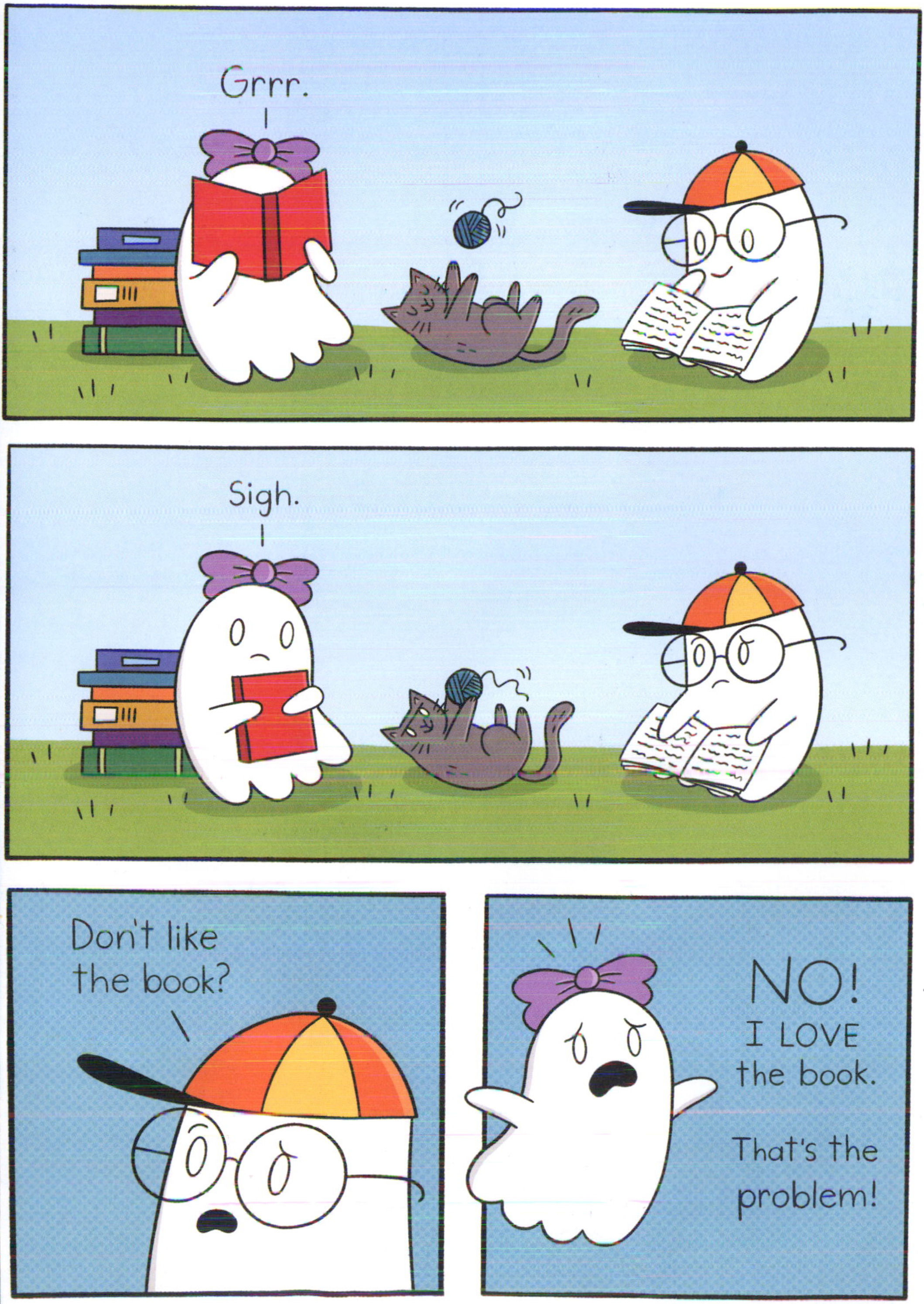
Grrr.
Sigh.
Don't like the book?
NO! I LOVE the book.
That's the problem!

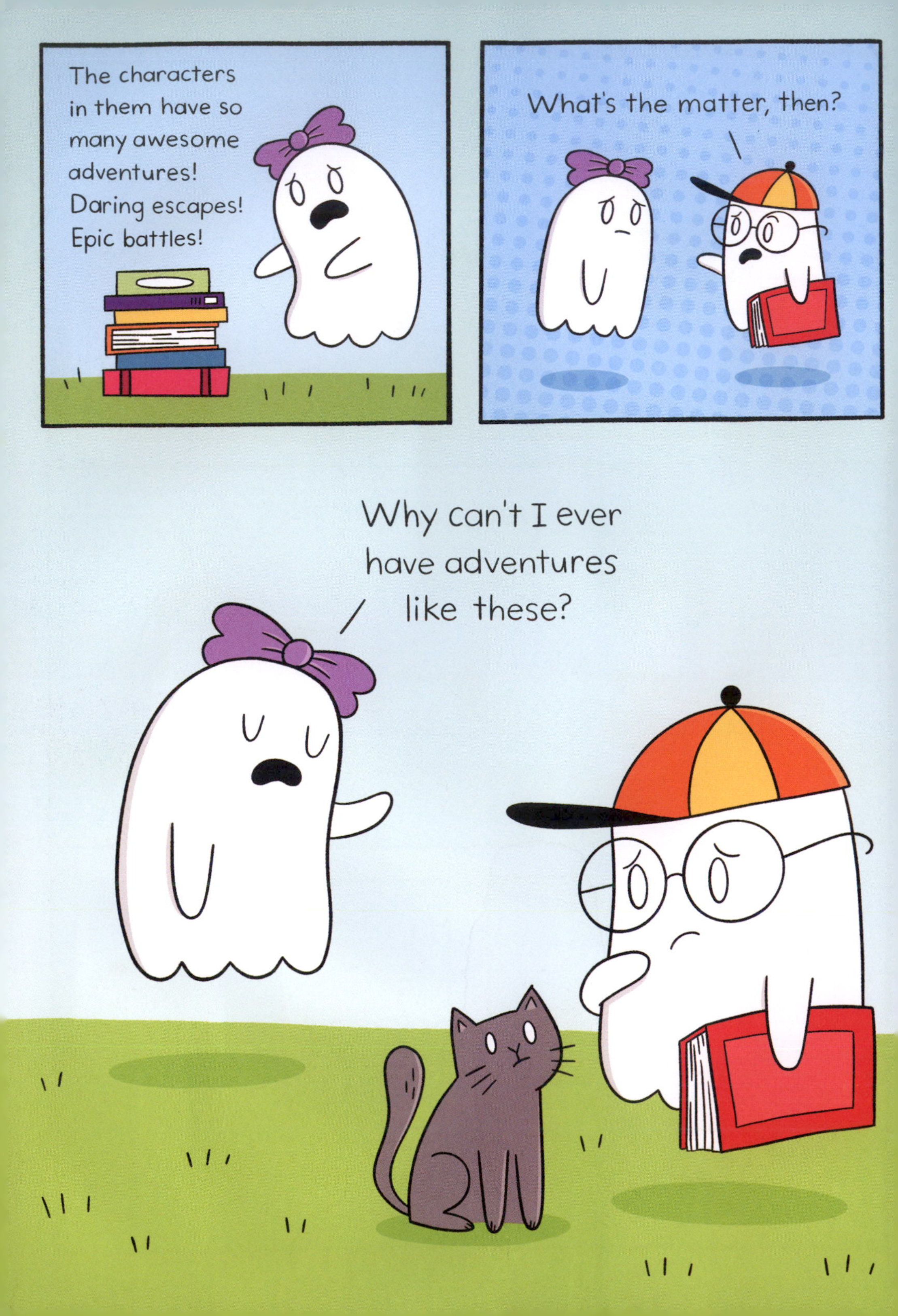

The characters in them have so many awesome adventures! Daring escapes! Epic battles!
What's the matter, then?
Why can't I ever have adventures like these?

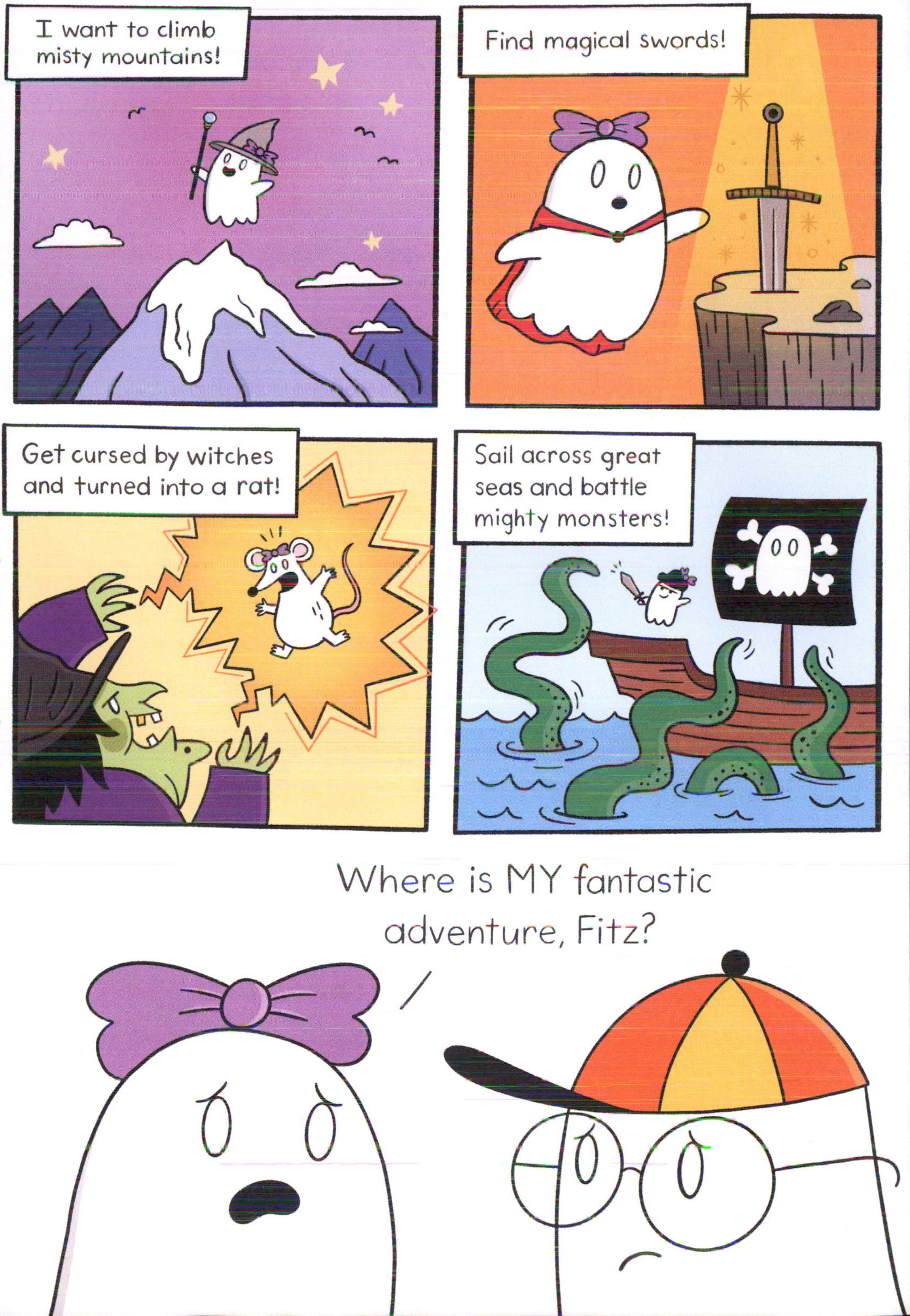
I want to climb misty mountains!
Find magical swords!
Get cursed by witches and turned into a rat!
Sail across great seas and battle mighty monsters!
Where is MY fantastic adventure, Fitz?

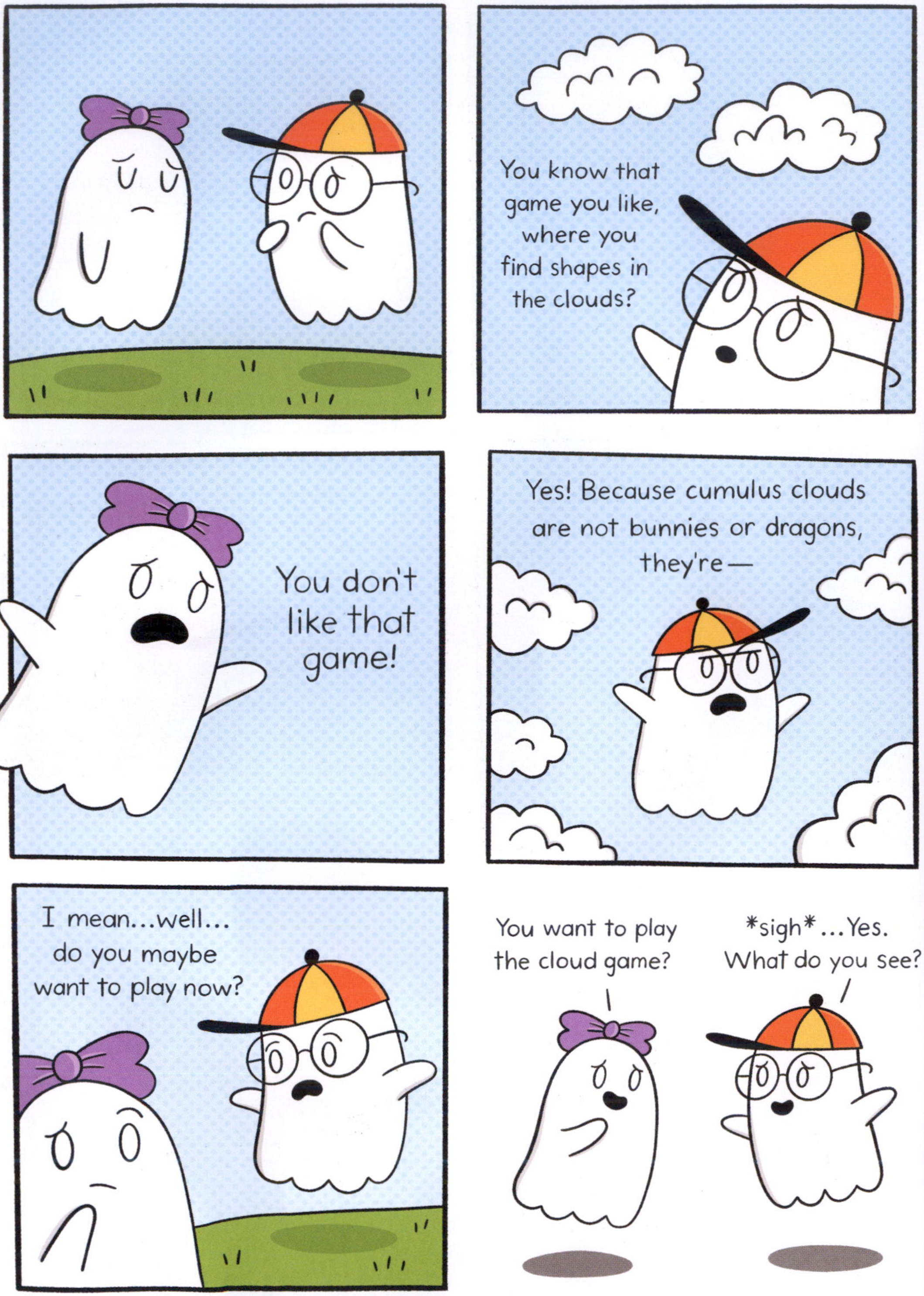
You know that game you like, where you find shapes in the clouds?
You don't like that game!
Yes! Because cumulus clouds are not bunnies or dragons, they're—
I mean...well... do you maybe want to play now?
You want to play the cloud game?
sigh...Yes. What do you see?

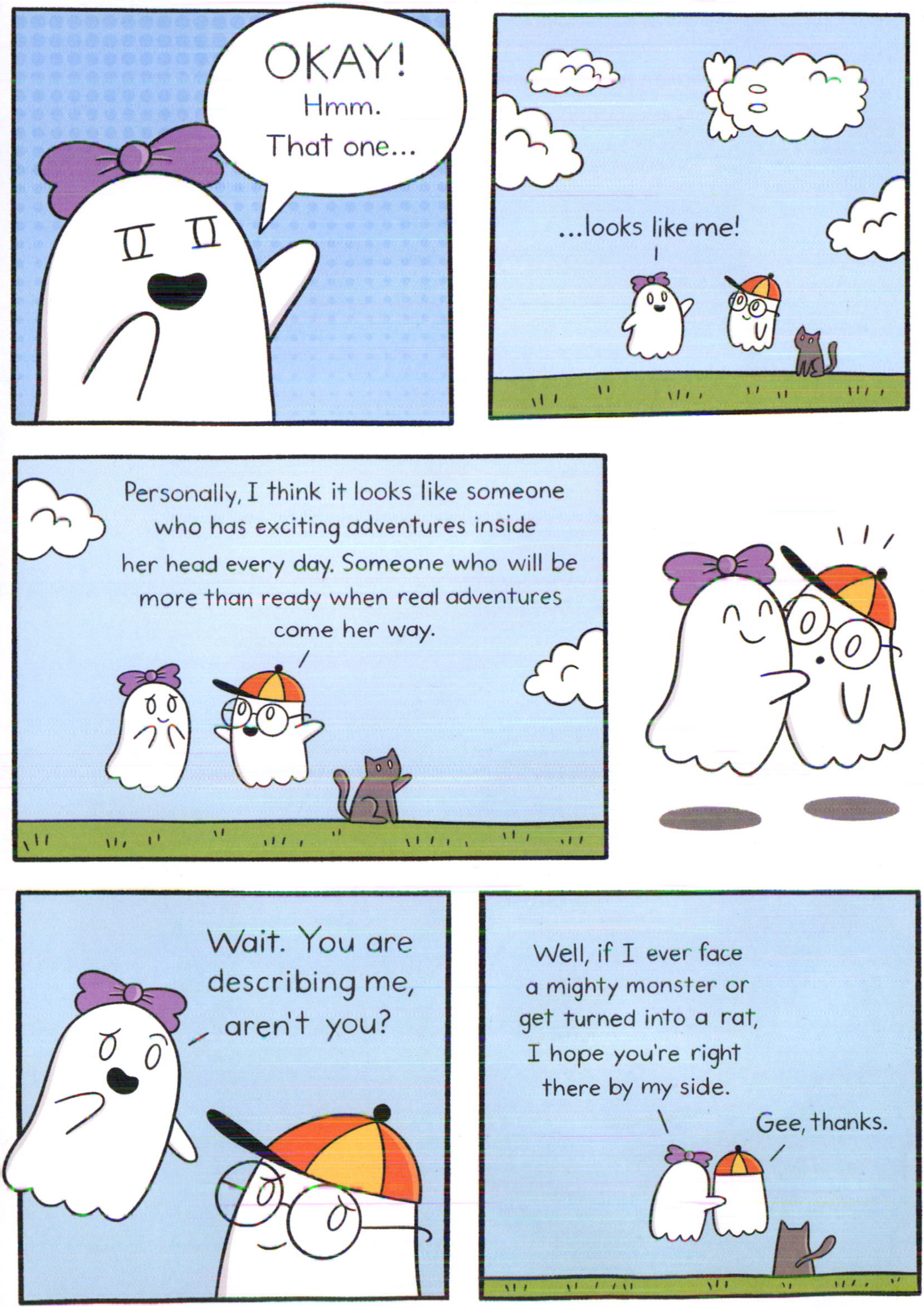
OKAY! Hmm. That one...
...looks like me!
Personally, I think it looks like someone who has exciting adventures inside her head every day. Someone who will be more than ready when real adventures come her way.
Wait. You are describing me, aren't you?
Well, if I ever face a mighty monster or get turned into a rat, I hope you're right there by my side.
Gee, thanks.

BOOOM!

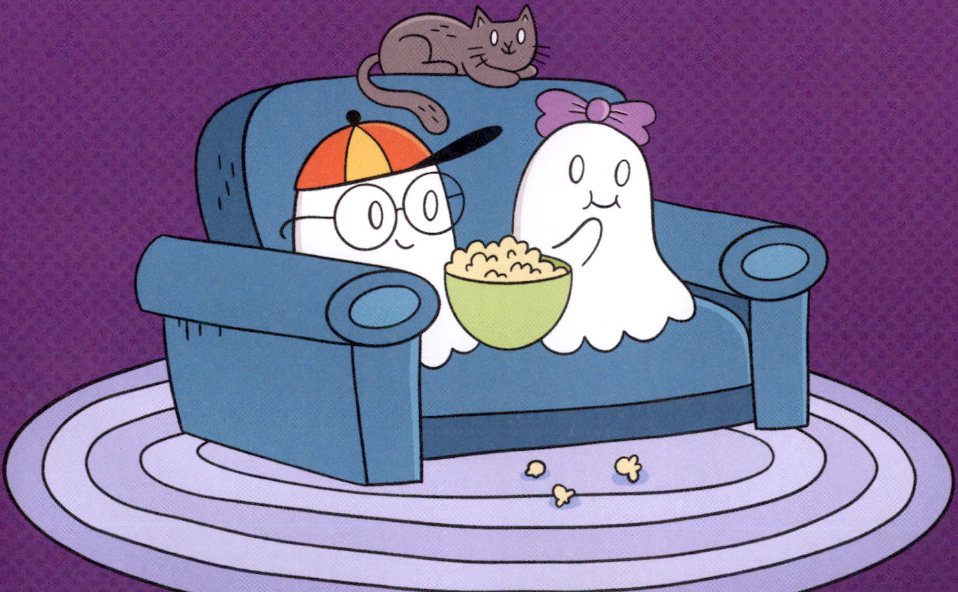

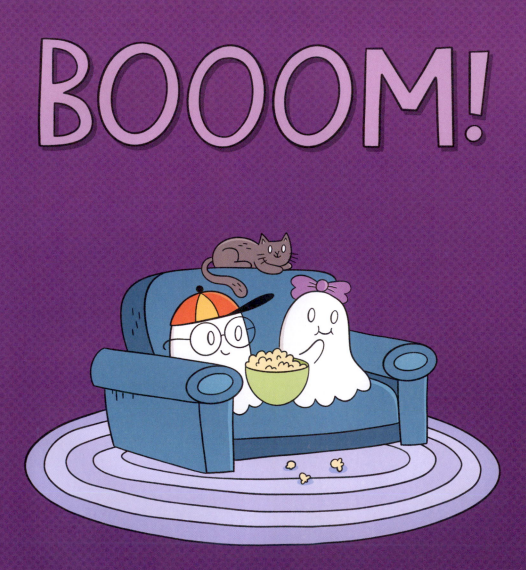

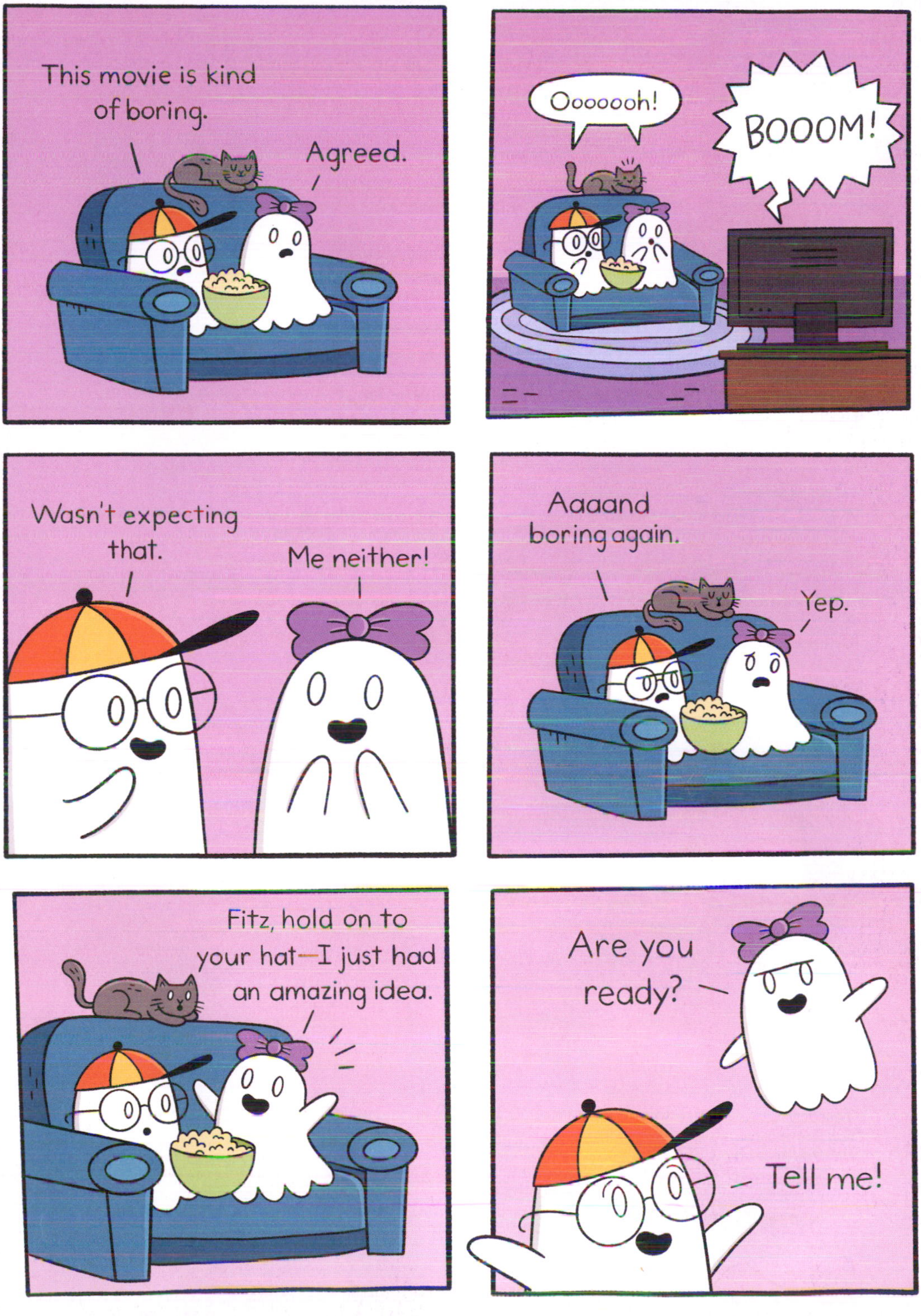
This movie is kind of boring.
Agreed.
Ooooooh!
BOOOM!
Wasn't expecting that.
Me neither!
Aaaand boring again.
Yep.
Fitz, hold on to your hat—I just had an amazing idea.
Are you ready?
Tell me!

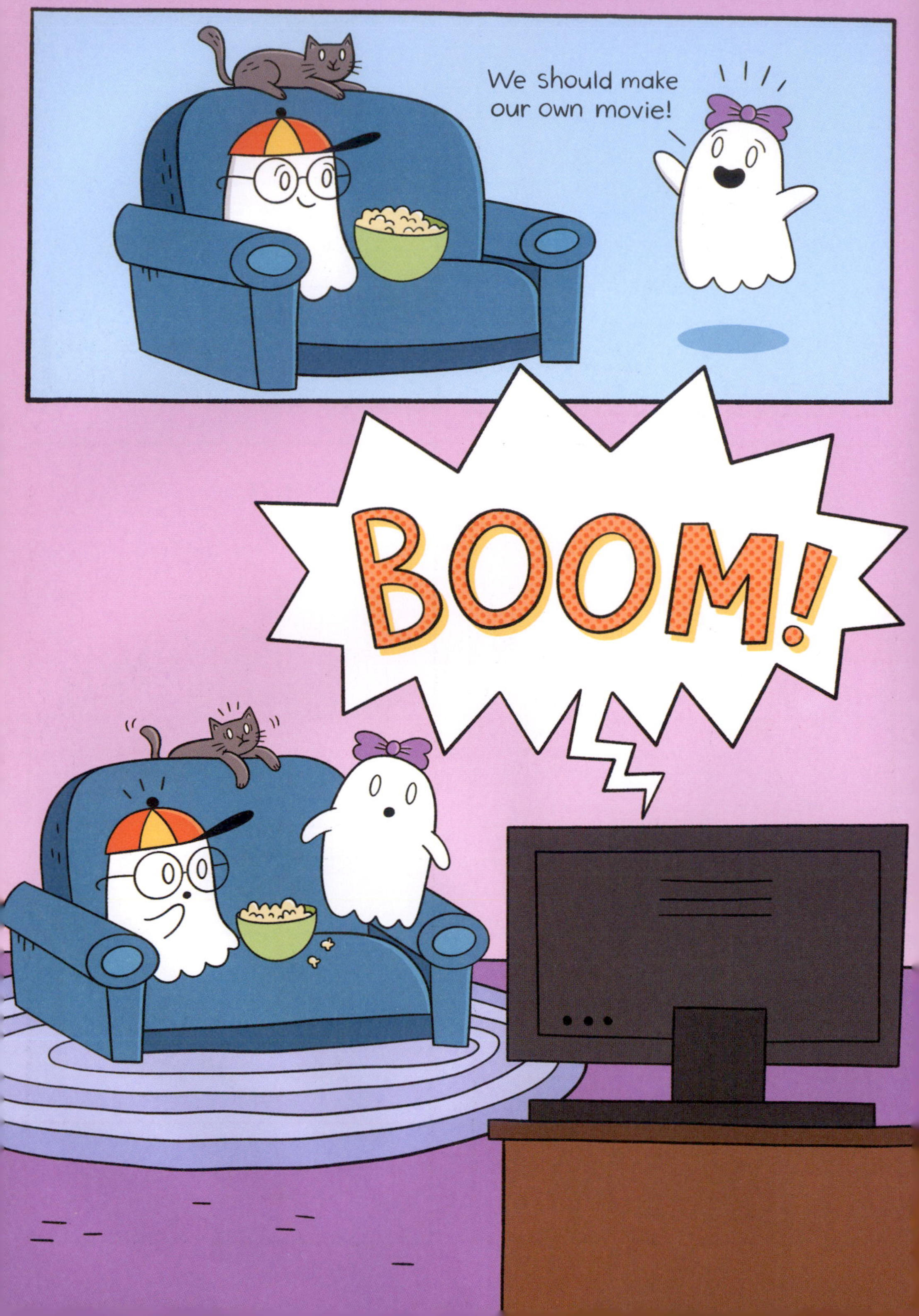
We should make our own movie!
BOOM!

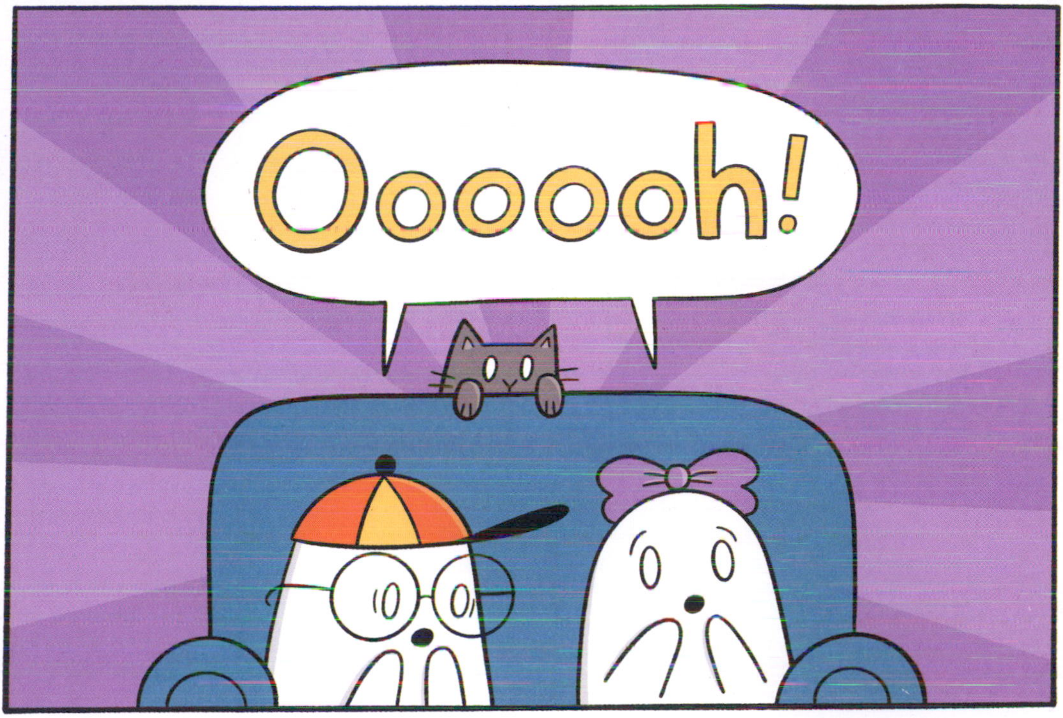
Oooooh!

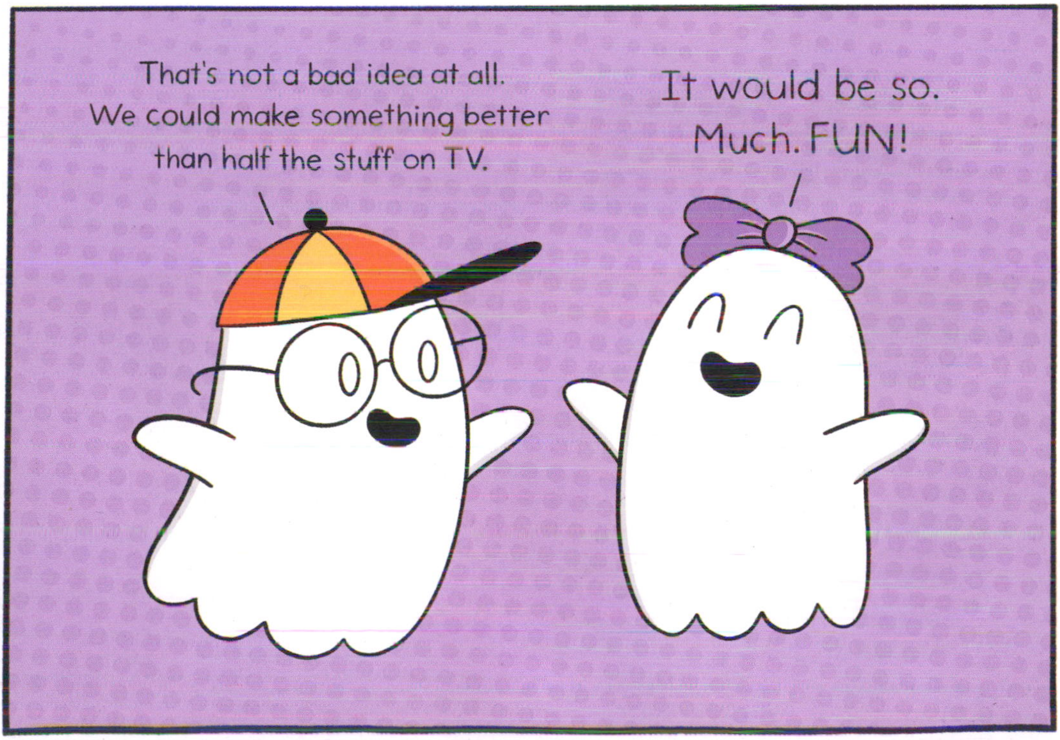
That's not a bad idea at all.
We could make something better
than half the stuff on TV.
It would be so.
Much. FUN!

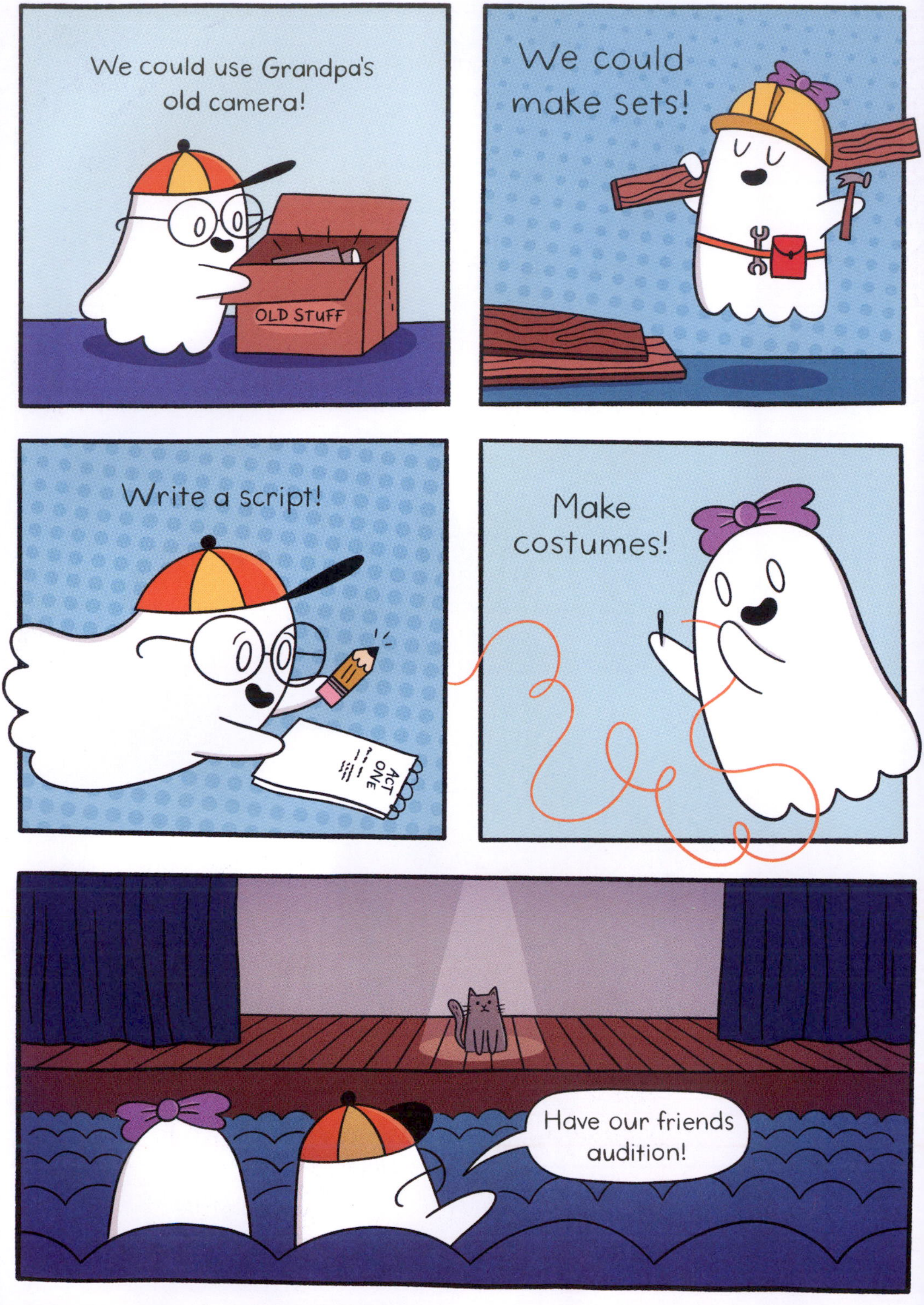
We could use Grandpa's old camera!
OLD STUFF
We could make sets!
Write a script!
ACT ONE
Make costumes!
Have our friends audition!

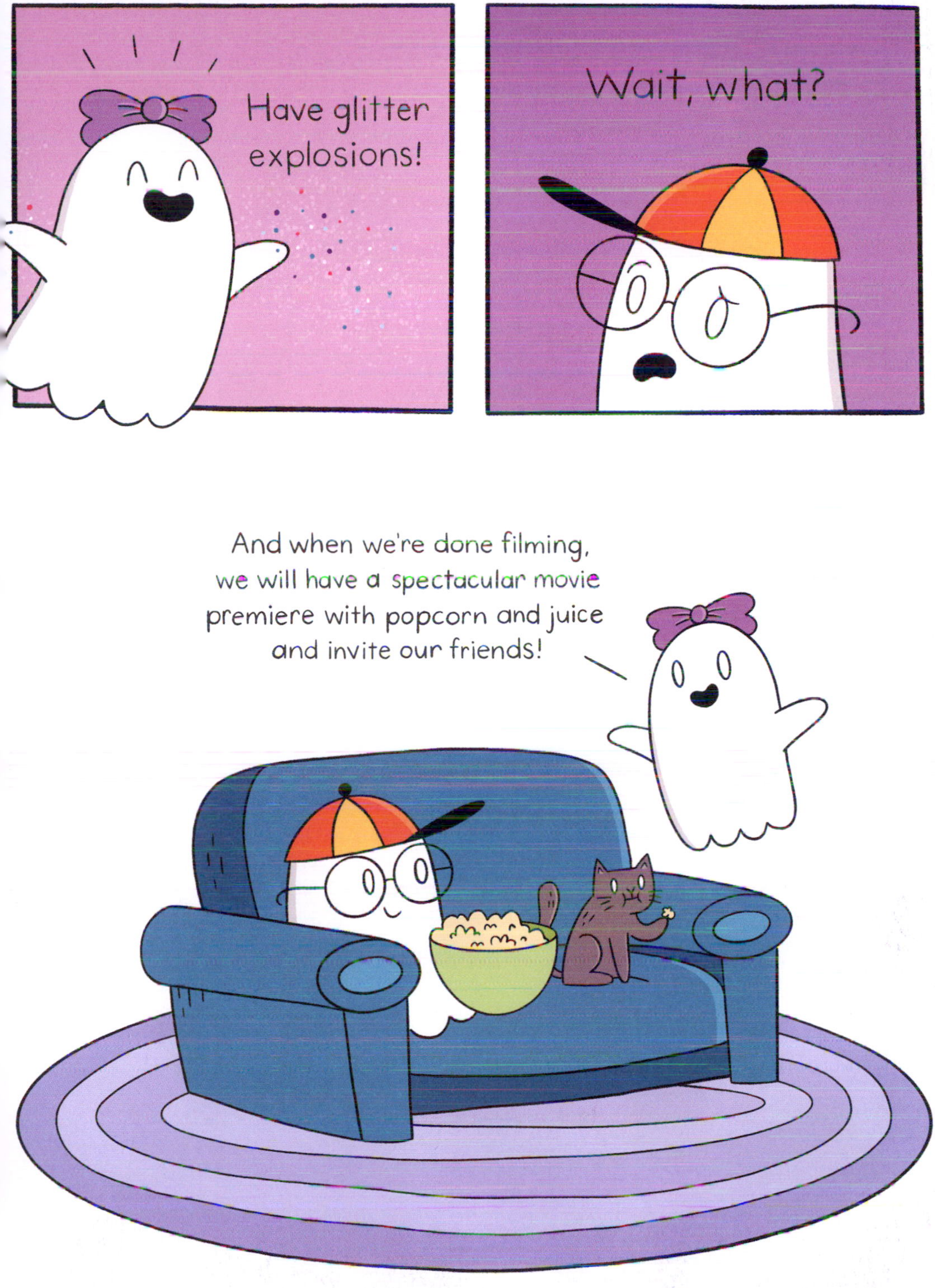
Have glitter explosions!
Wait, what?
And when we're done filming, we will have a spectacular movie premiere with popcorn and juice and invite our friends!

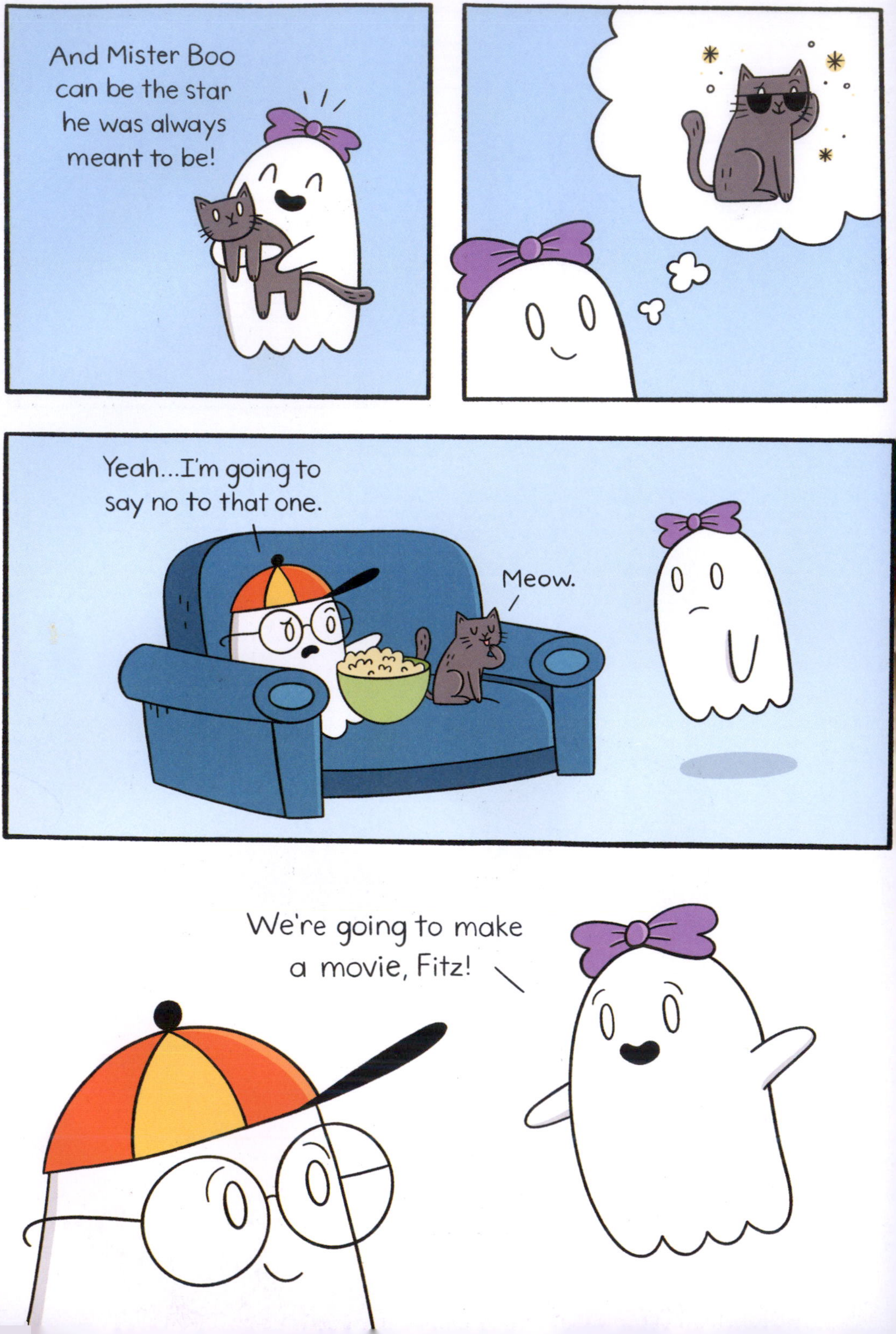
And Mister Boo can be the star he was always meant to be!
Yeah...I'm going to say no to that one.
Meow.
We're going to make a movie, Fitz!

Movie!

Movie!

Movie!

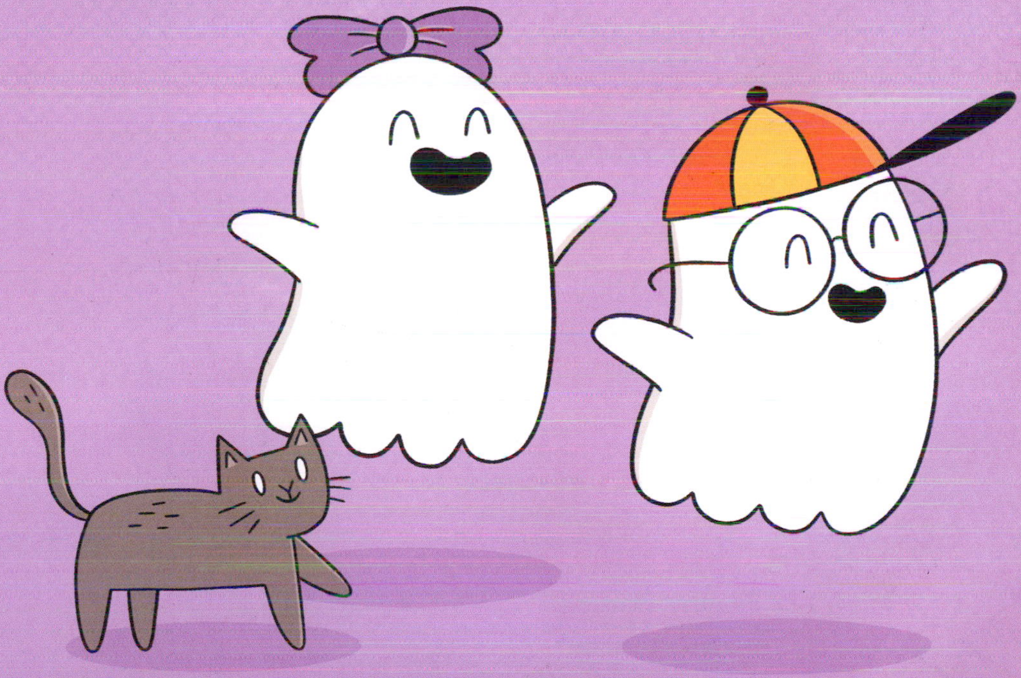

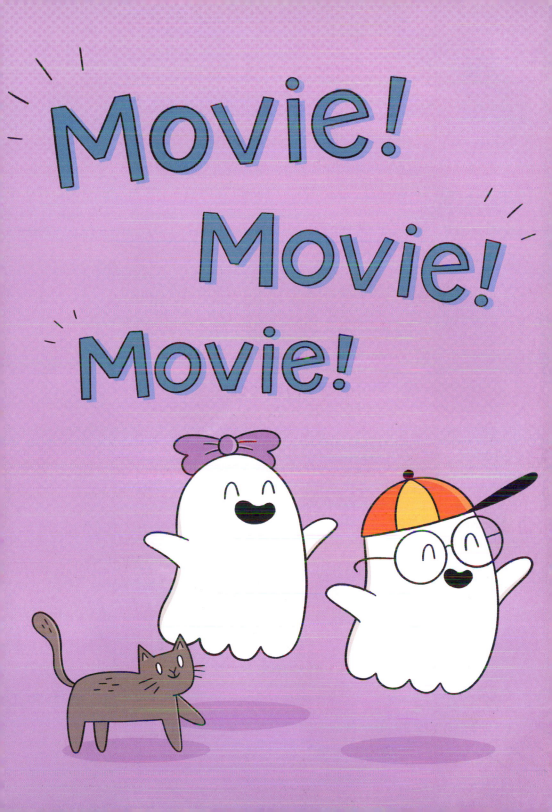

Write Now

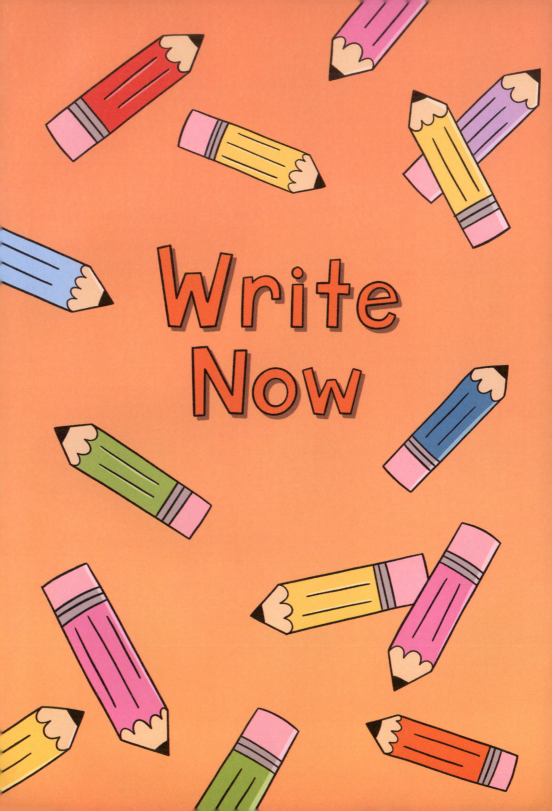

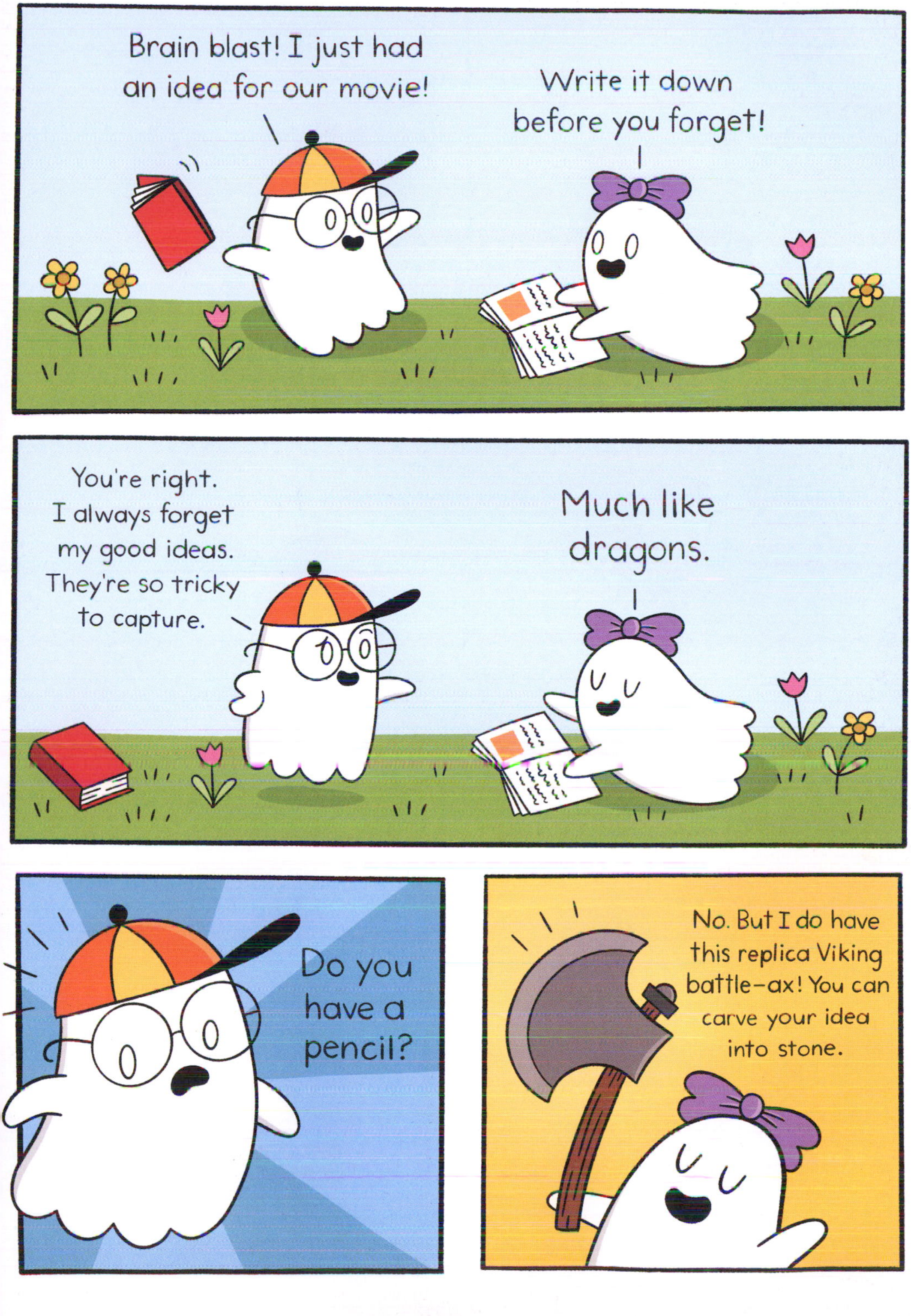
Brain blast! I just had an idea for our movie!
Write it down before you forget!
You're right. I always forget my good ideas. They're so tricky to capture.
Much like dragons.
Do you have a pencil?
No. But I do have this replica Viking battle-ax! You can carve your idea into stone.

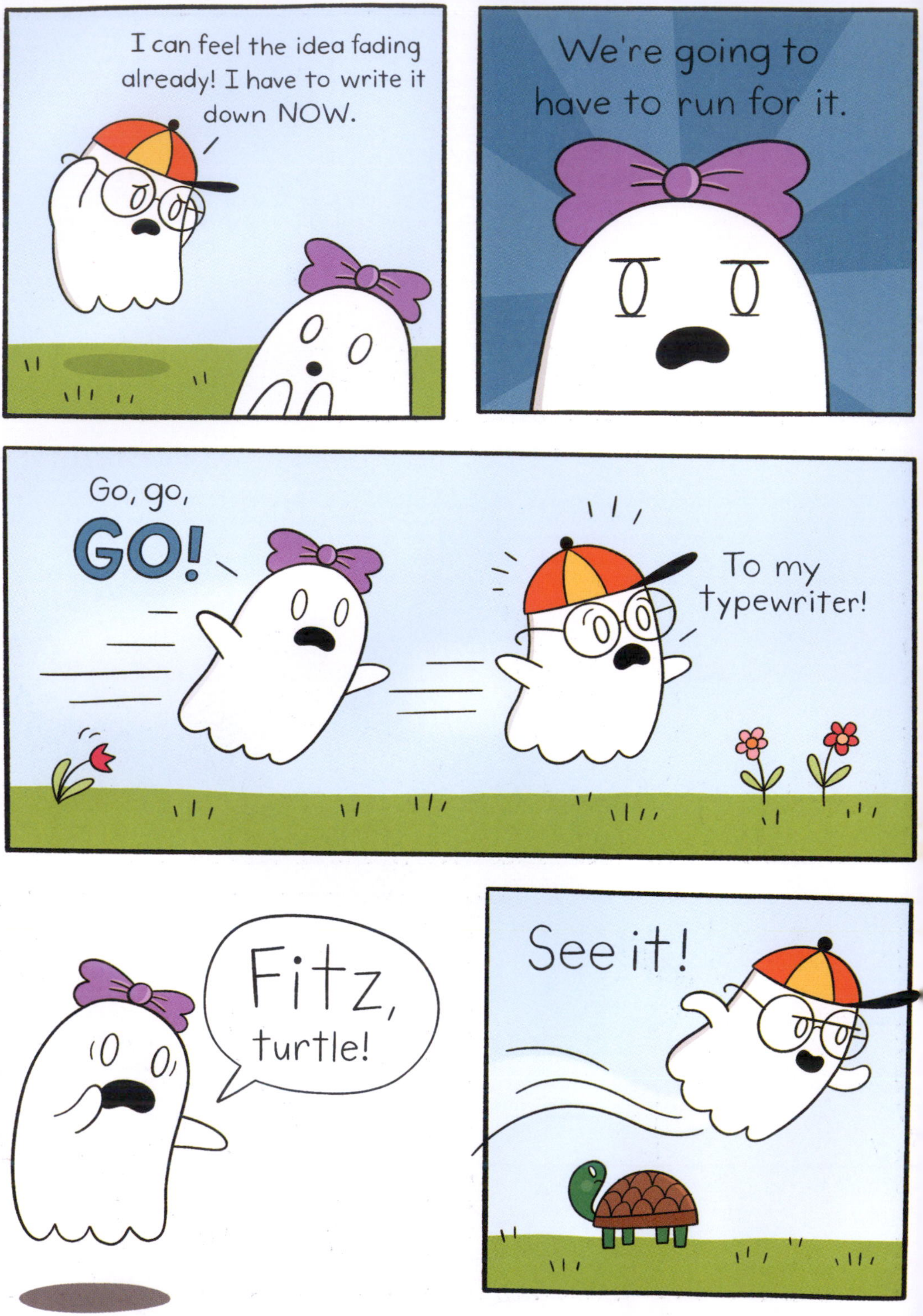

I can feel the idea fading already! I have to write it down NOW.
We're going to have to run for it.
Go, go, GO!
To my typewriter!
Fitz, turtle!
See it!

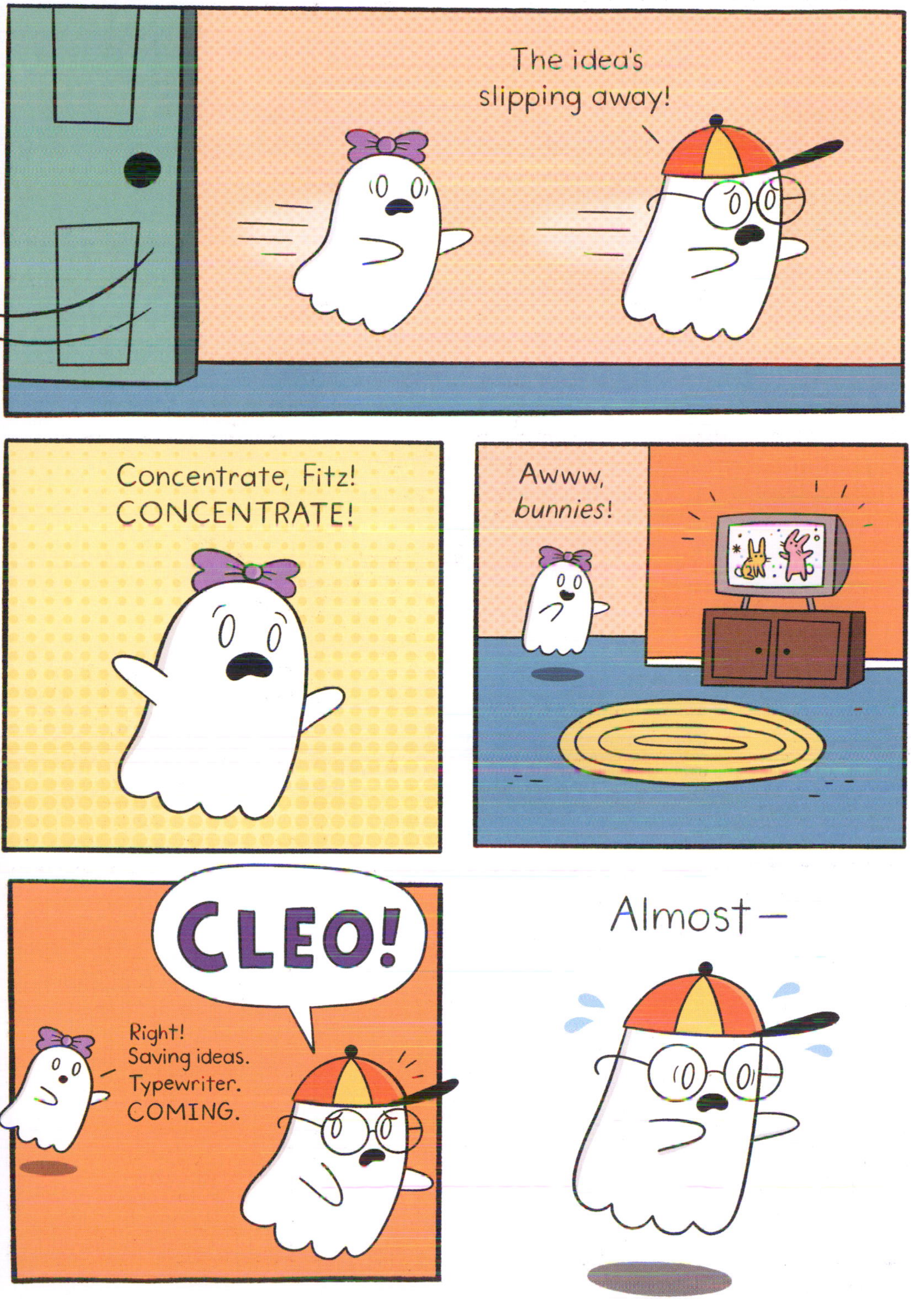
The idea's slipping away!
Concentrate, Fitz! CONCENTRATE!
Awww, *bunnies*!
CLEO!
Right! Saving ideas. Typewriter. COMING.
Almost—

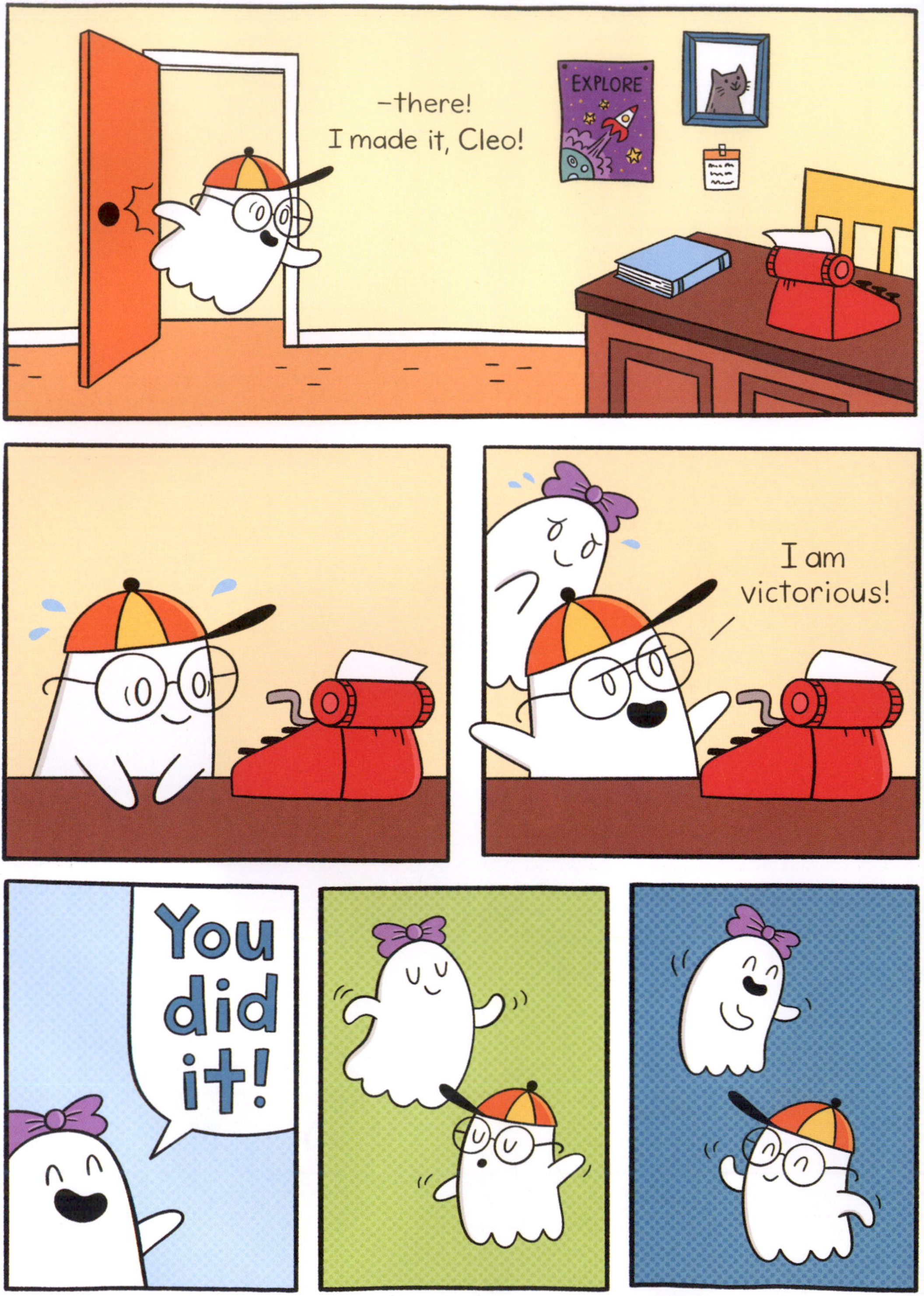

–there!
I made it, Cleo!
EXPLORE
I am victorious!
You did it!

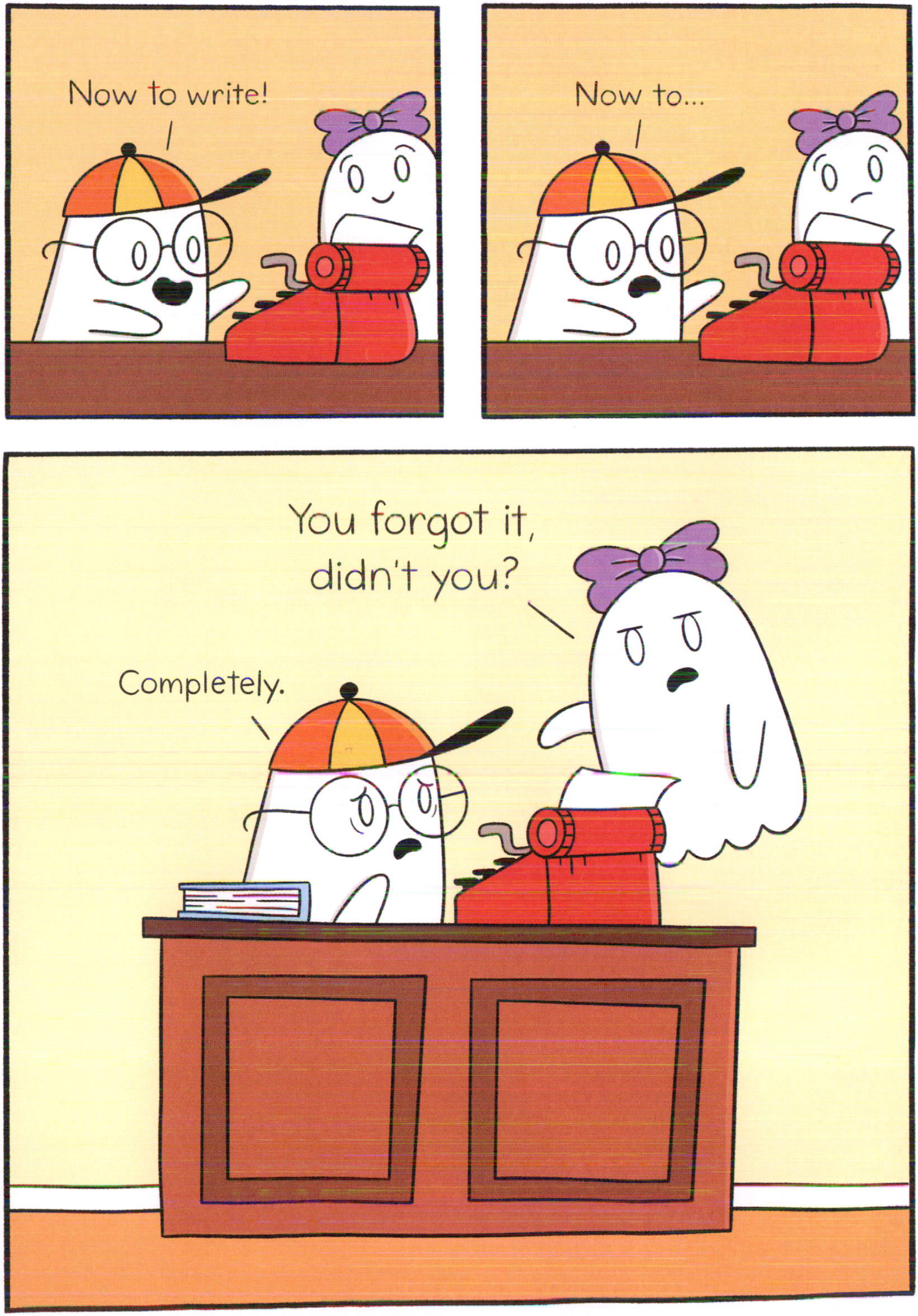
Now to write!
Now to...
You forgot it, didn't you?
Completely.

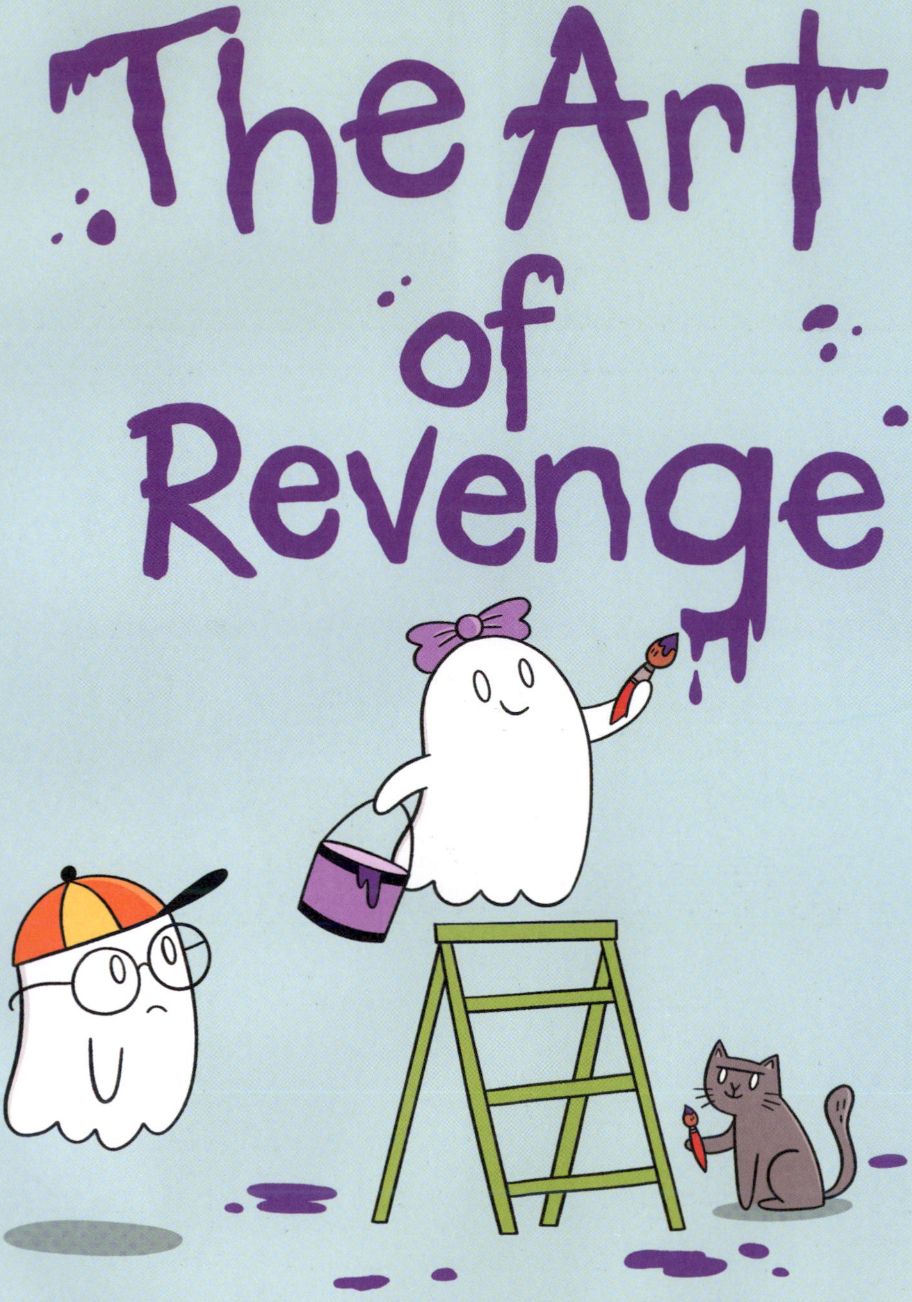
The Art
of
Revenge

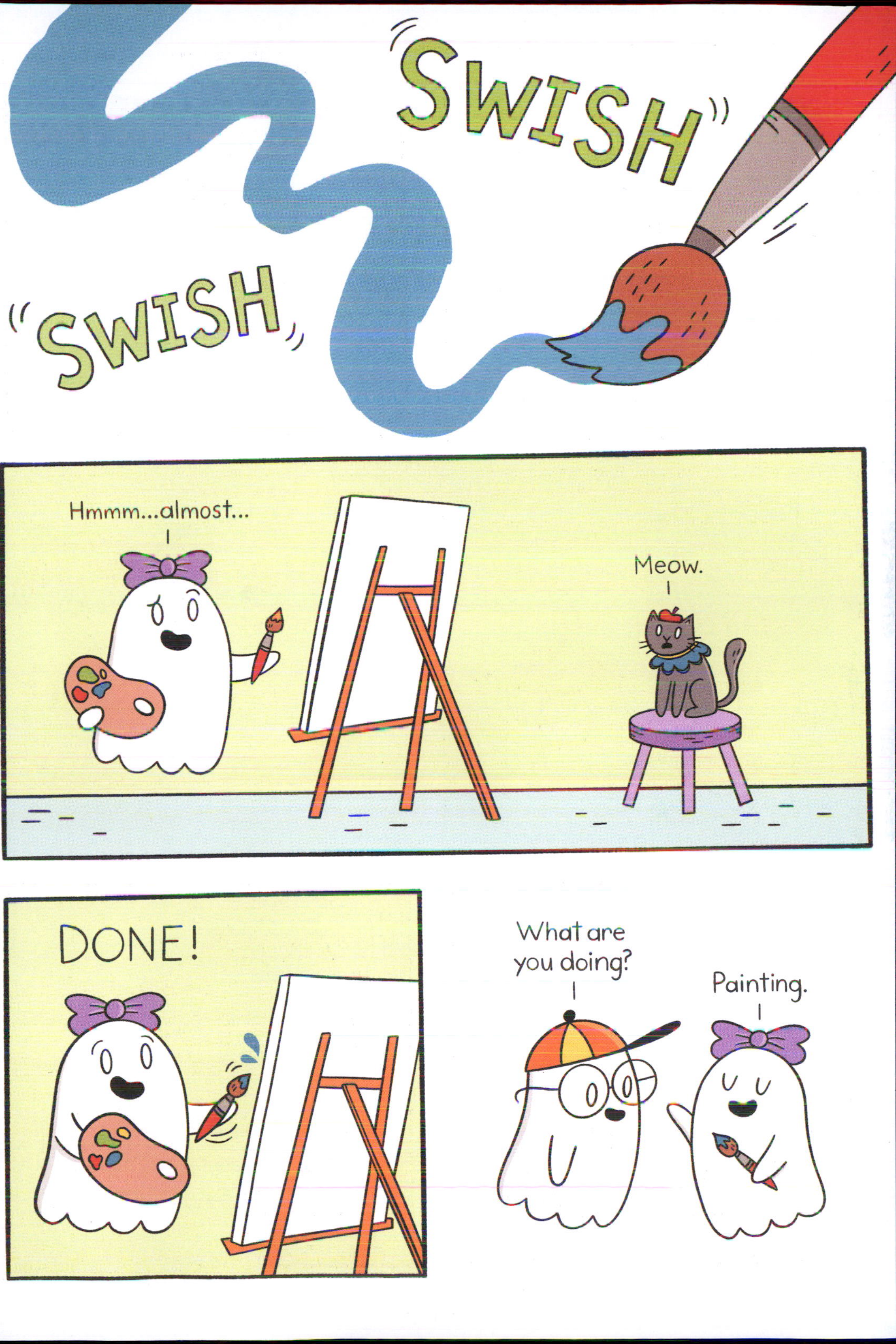
SWISH
SWISH
Hmmm...almost...
Meow.
DONE!
What are you doing?
Painting.

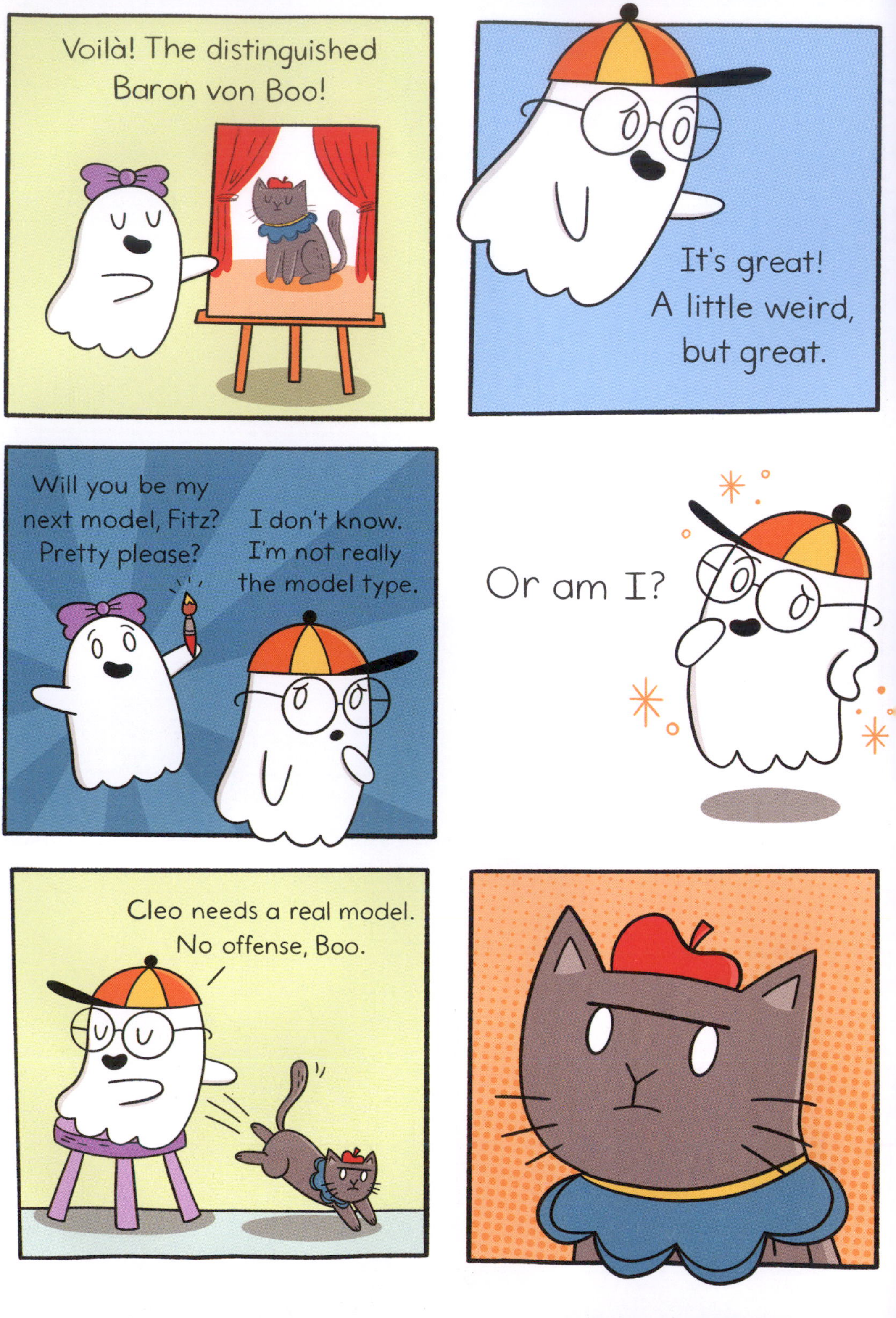
Voilà! The distinguished Baron von Boo!
It's great! A little weird, but great.
Will you be my next model, Fitz? Pretty please?
I don't know. I'm not really the model type.
Or am I?
Cleo needs a real model. No offense, Boo.

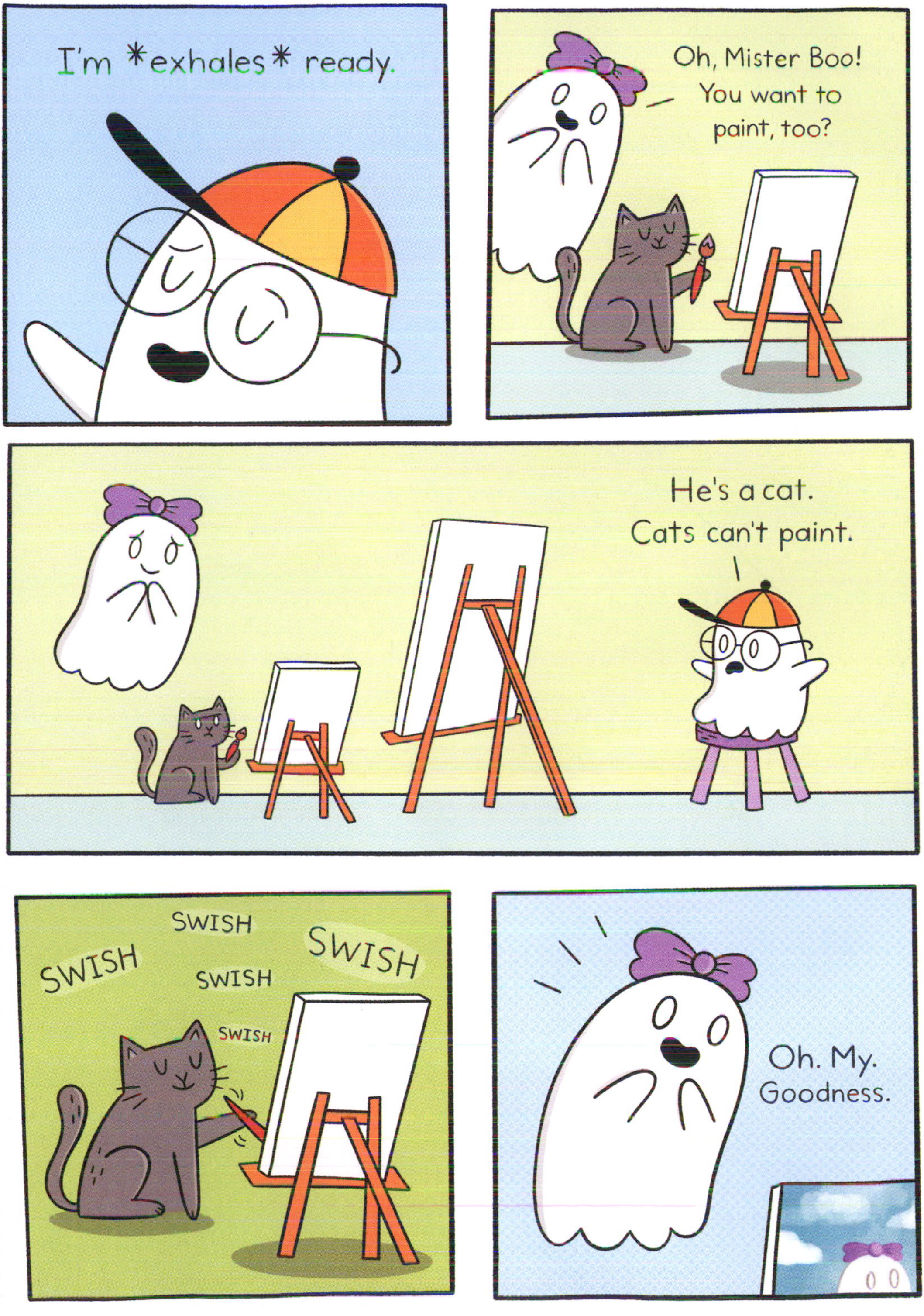
I'm *exhales* ready.
Oh, Mister Boo! You want to paint, too?
He's a cat. Cats can't paint.
SWISH
SWISH
SWISH
SWISH
SWISH
Oh. My. Goodness.

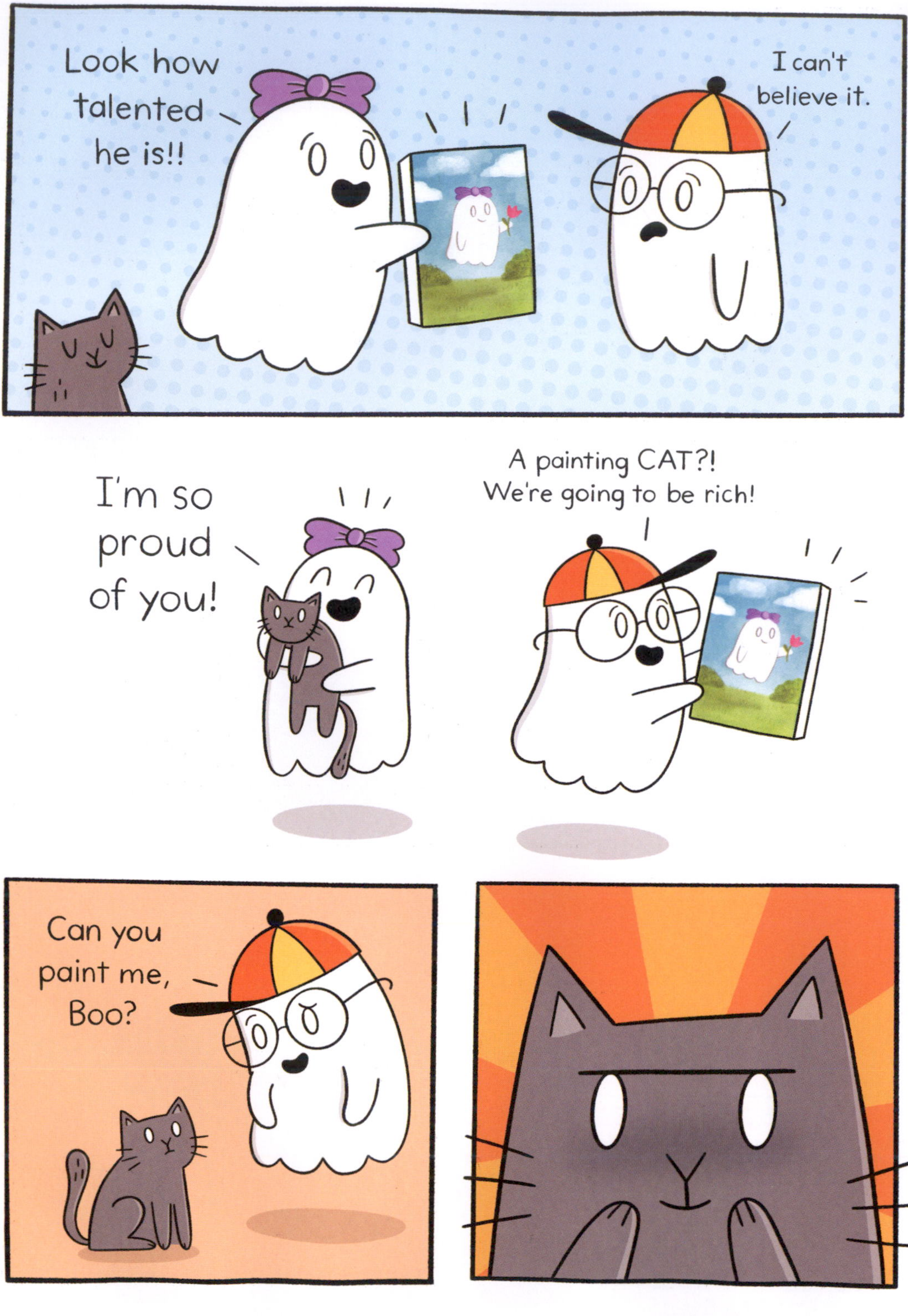
Look how talented he is!!
I can't believe it.
I'm so proud of you!
A painting CAT?! We're going to be rich!
Can you paint me, Boo?

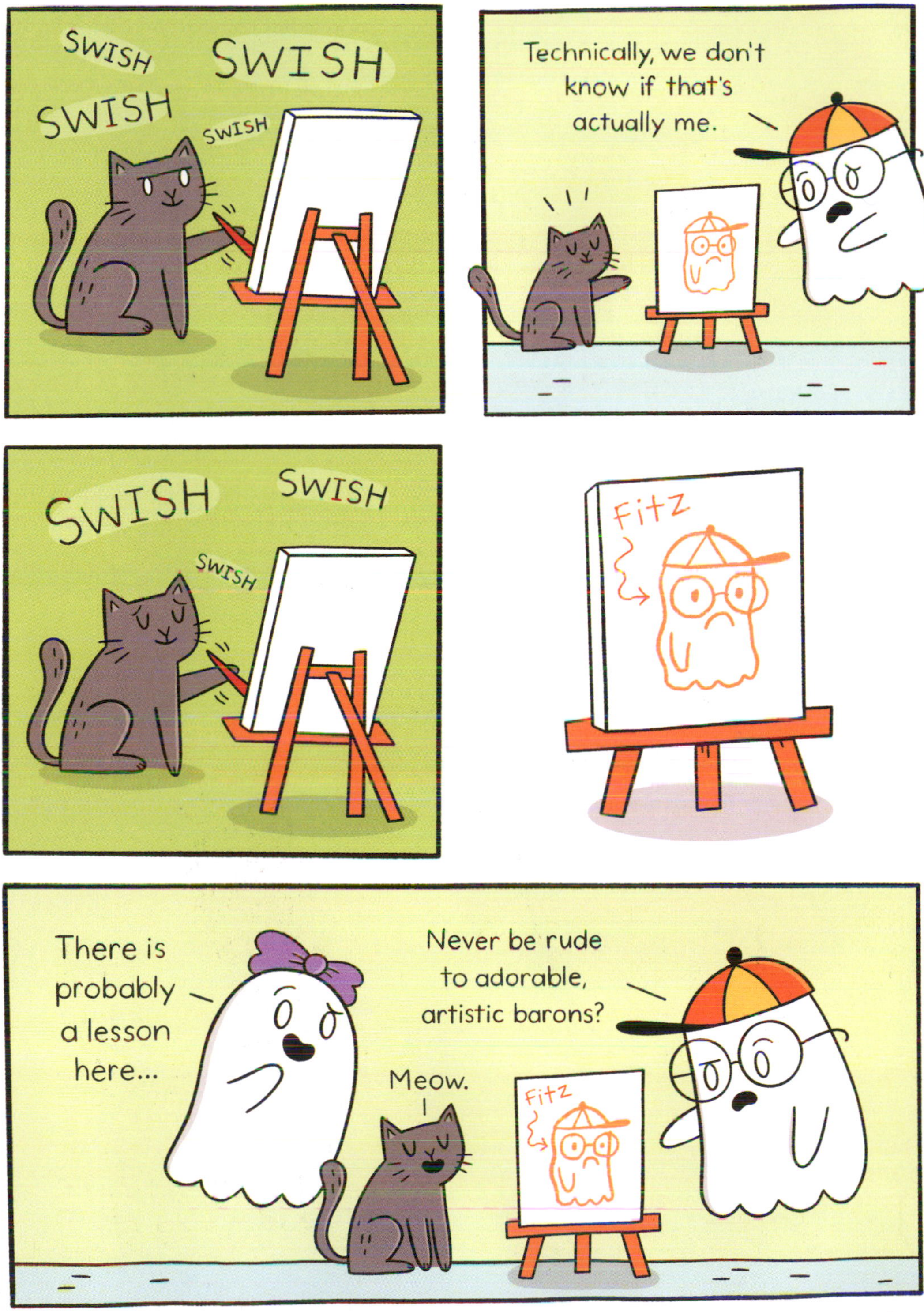
SWISH
SWISH
SWISH
SWISH
Technically, we don't know if that's actually me.
SWISH
SWISH
SWISH
Fitz
There is probably a lesson here...
Never be rude to adorable, artistic barons?
Meow.
Fitz

Once Upon a Time

No.

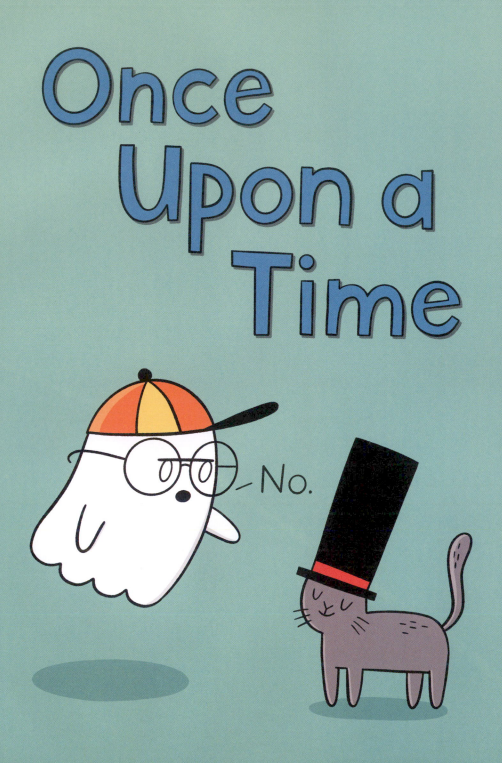

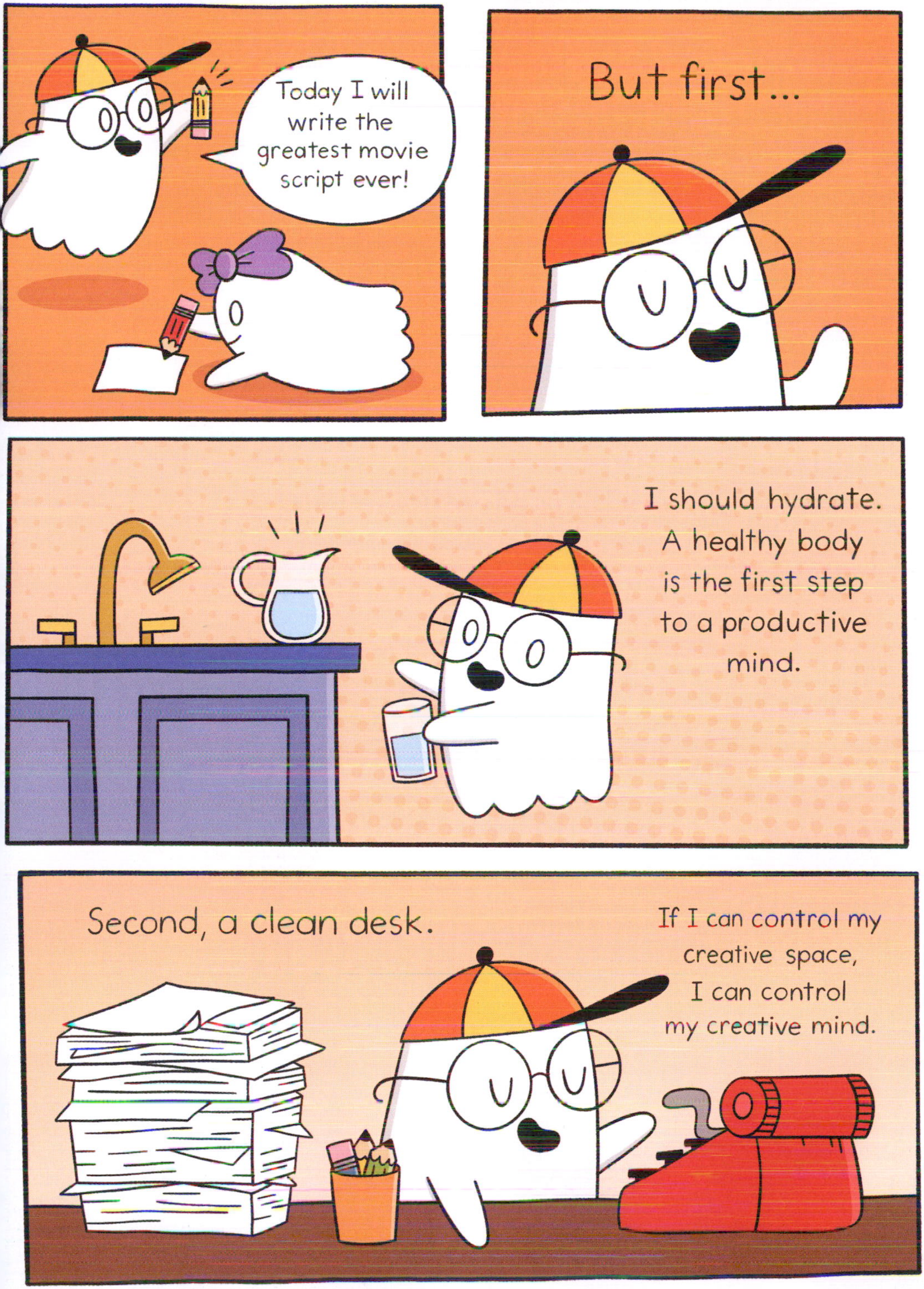
Today I will write the greatest movie script ever!
But first...
I should hydrate. A healthy body is the first step to a productive mind.
Second, a clean desk.
If I can control my creative space, I can control my creative mind.

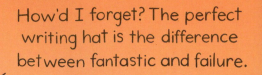

How'd I forget? The perfect writing hat is the difference between fantastic and failure.

No. No. No.

Maybe.

NO.

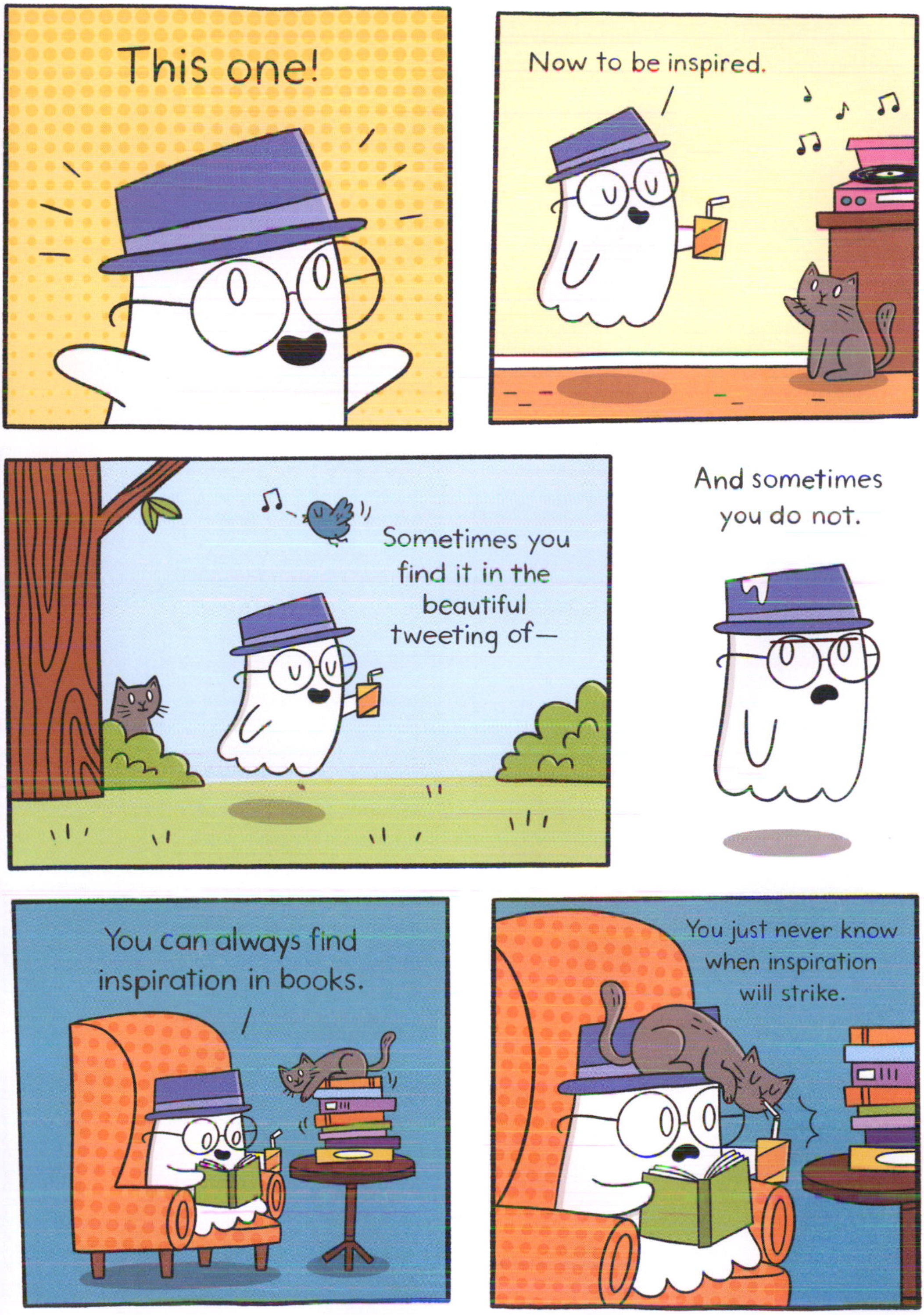
This one!
Now to be inspired.
Sometimes you find it in the beautiful tweeting of—
And sometimes you do not.
You can always find inspiration in books.
You just never know when inspiration will strike.

Then, and only then, is the
writer ready to write.

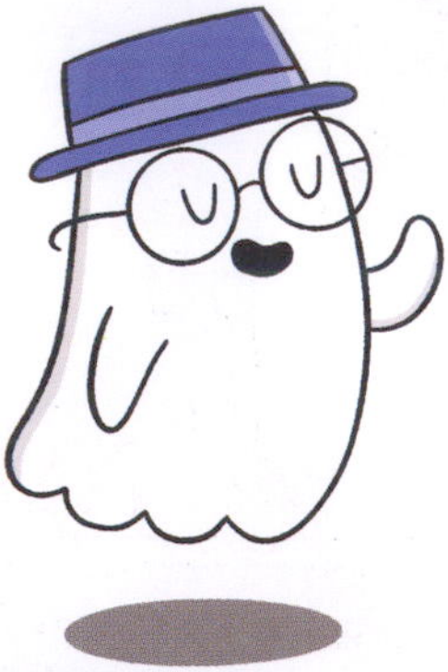

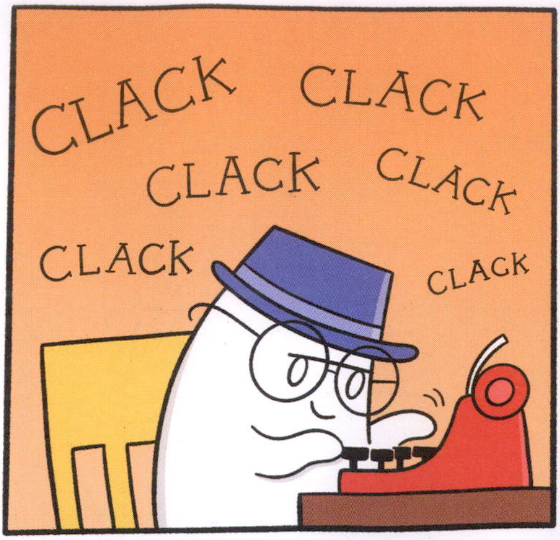
CLACK CLACK
CLACK CLACK
CLACK
CLACK

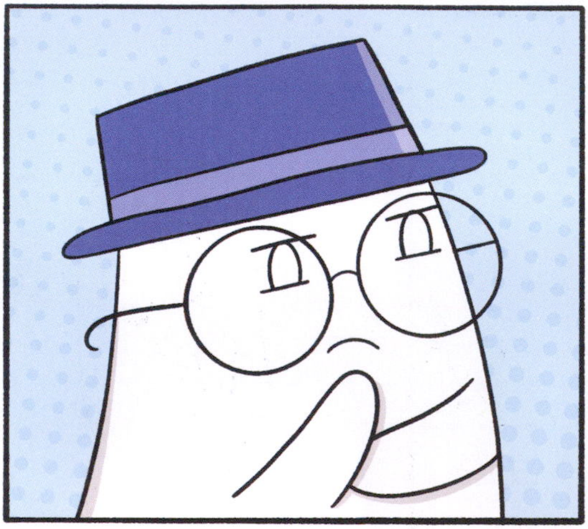

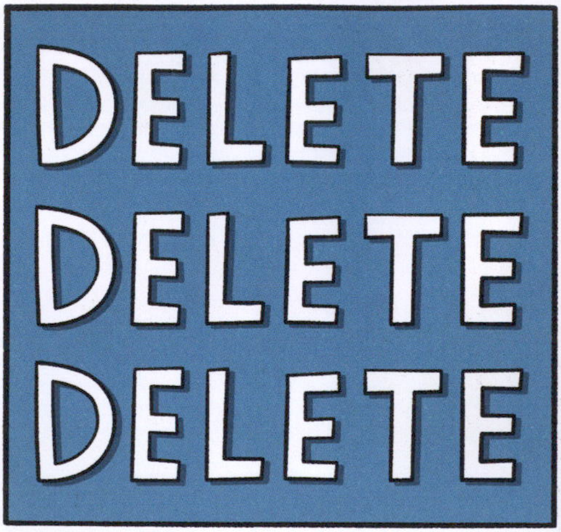
DELETE
DELETE
DELETE

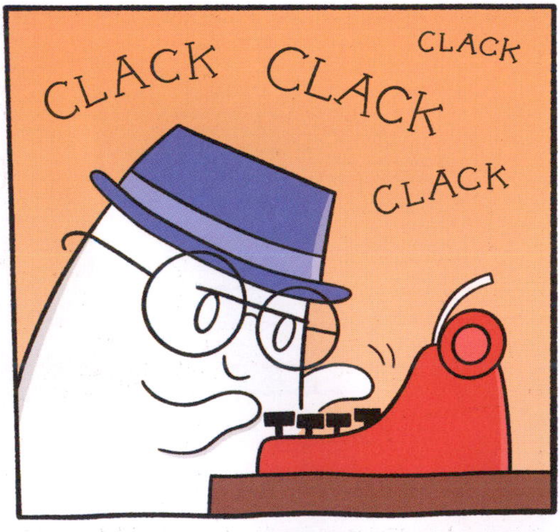
CLACK CLACK
CLACK
CLACK

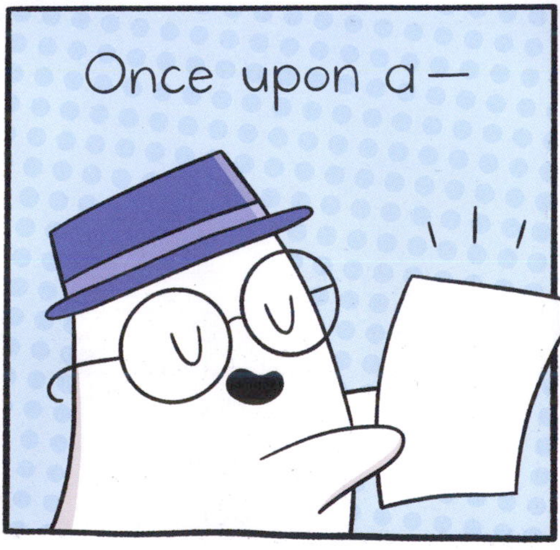
Once upon a—

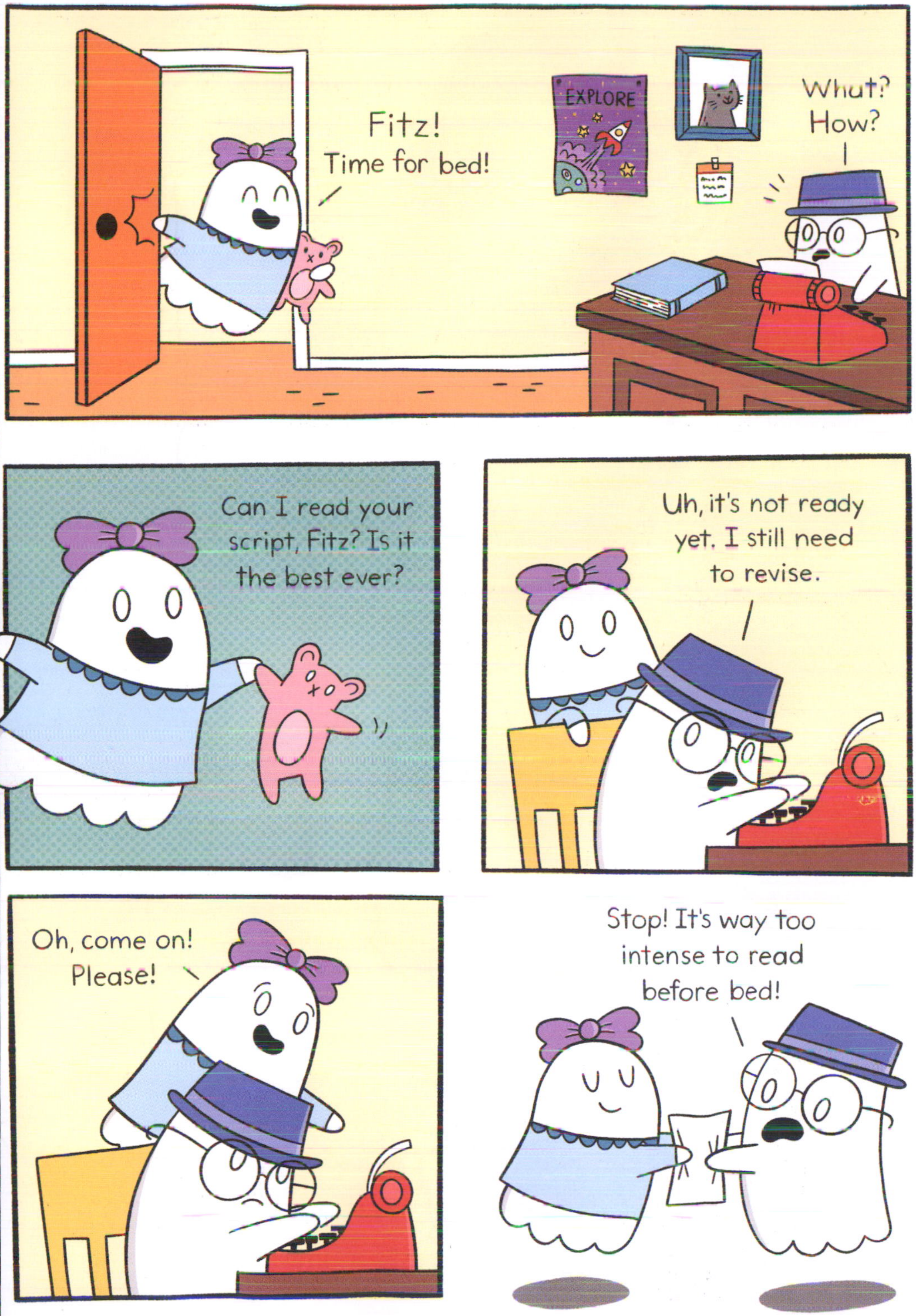

Fitz!
Time for bed!
EXPLORE
What? How?
Can I read your script, Fitz? Is it the best ever?
Uh, it's not ready yet. I still need to revise.
Oh, come on! Please!
Stop! It's way too intense to read before bed!

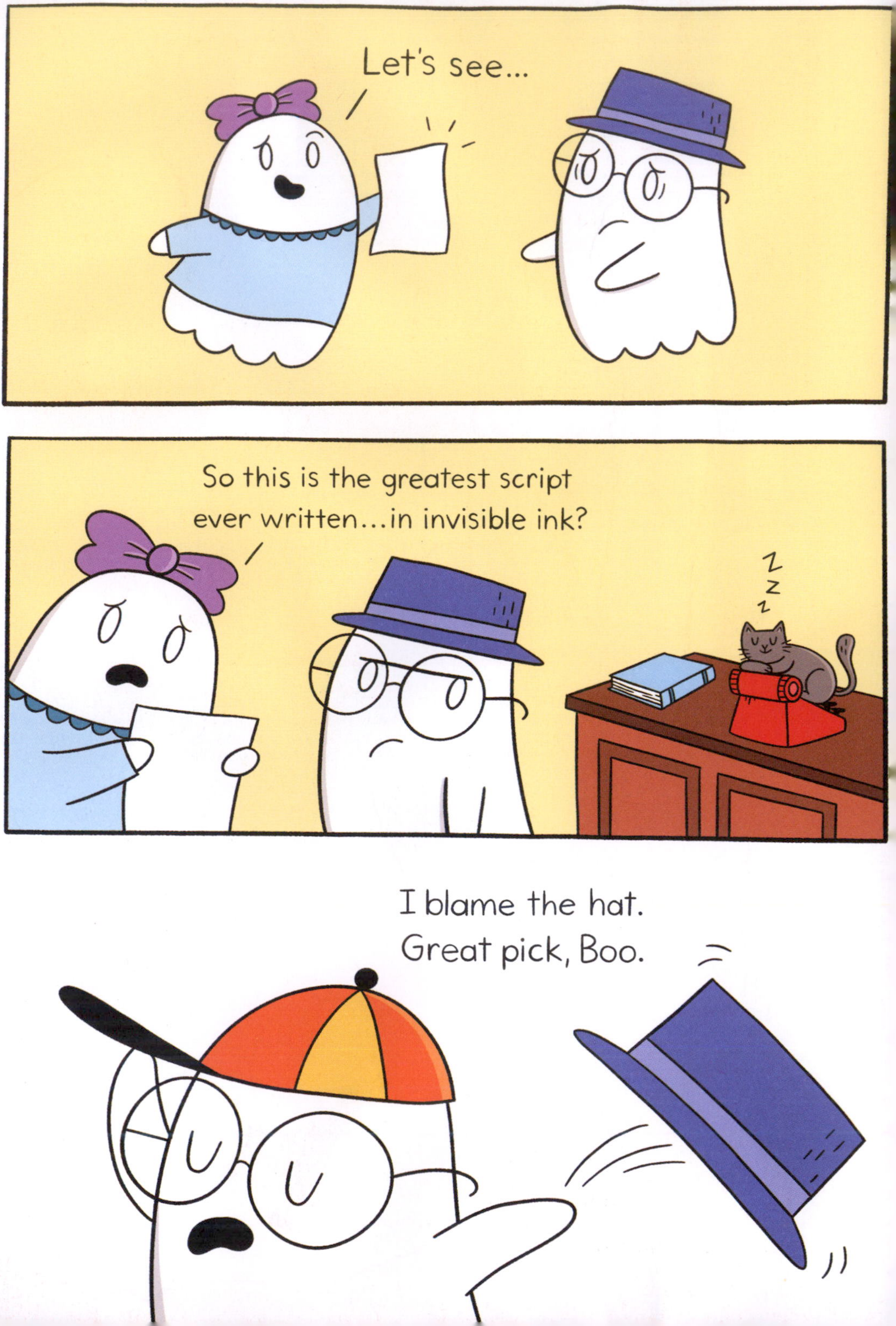
Let's see...
So this is the greatest script ever written...in invisible ink?
I blame the hat. Great pick, Boo.

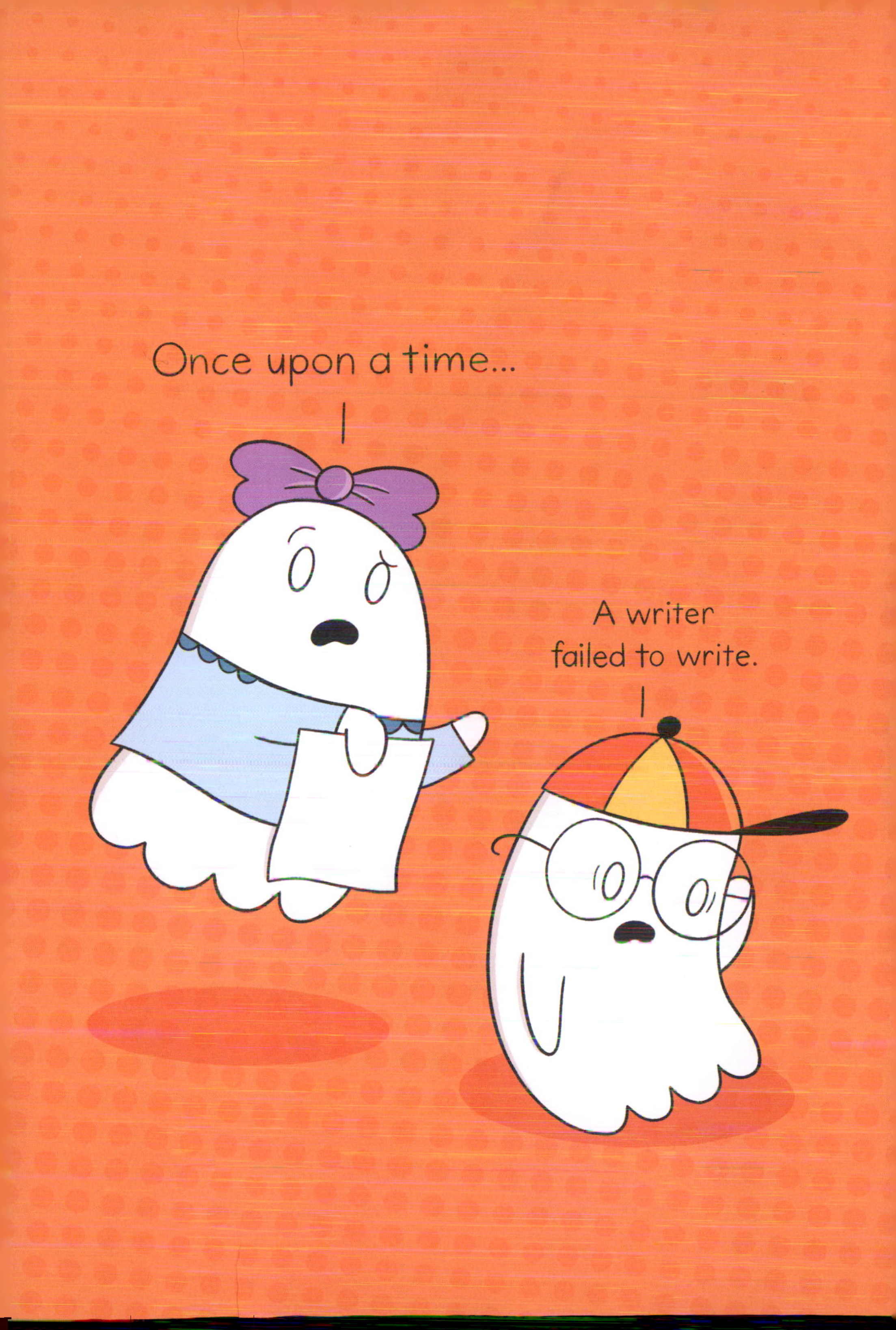
Once upon a time...
A writer
failed to write.

Rock
Paper
Scissors

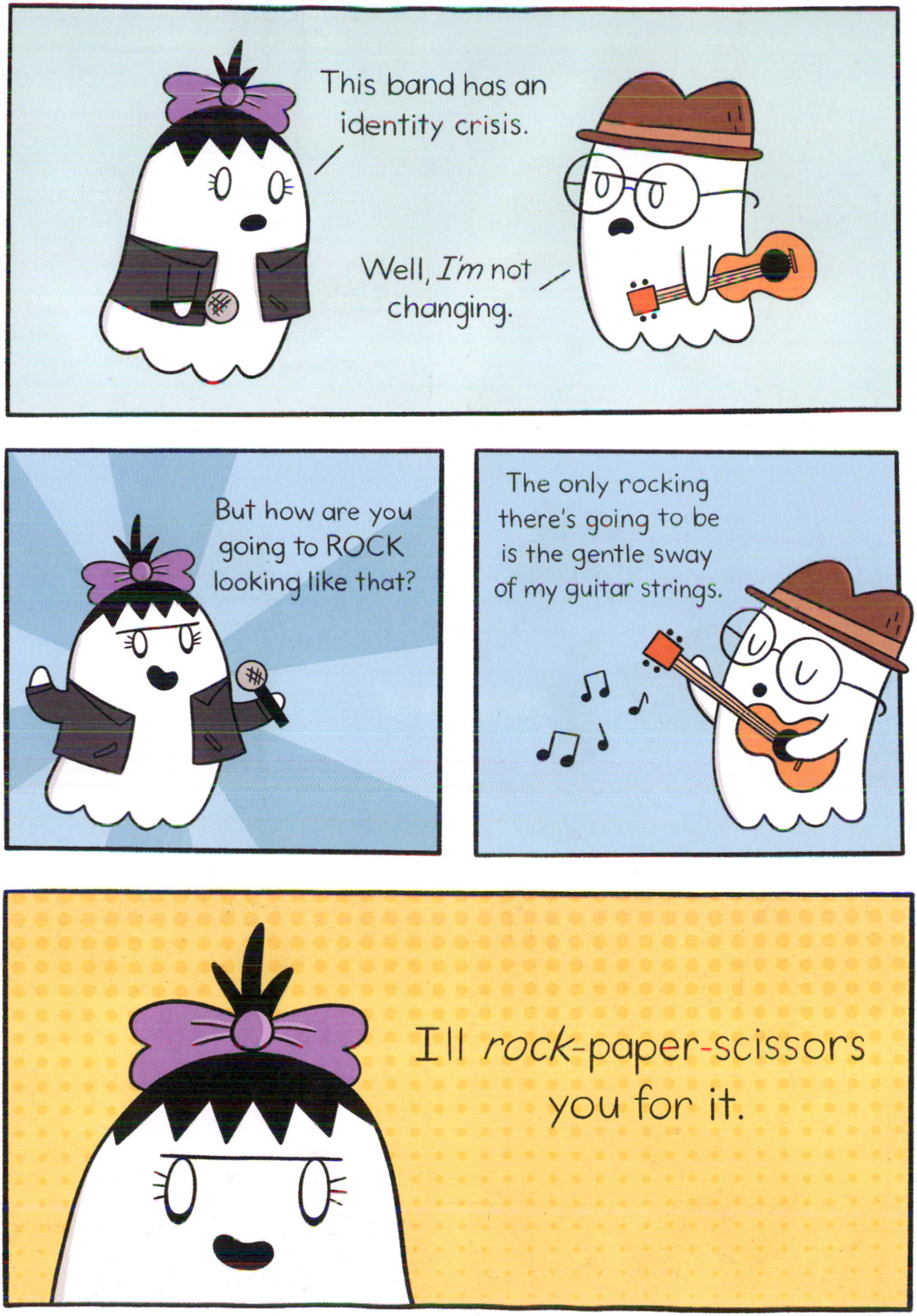
This band has an identity crisis.
Well, *I'm* not changing.
But how are you going to ROCK looking like that?
The only rocking there's going to be is the gentle sway of my guitar strings.
Ill *rock*-paper-scissors you for it.

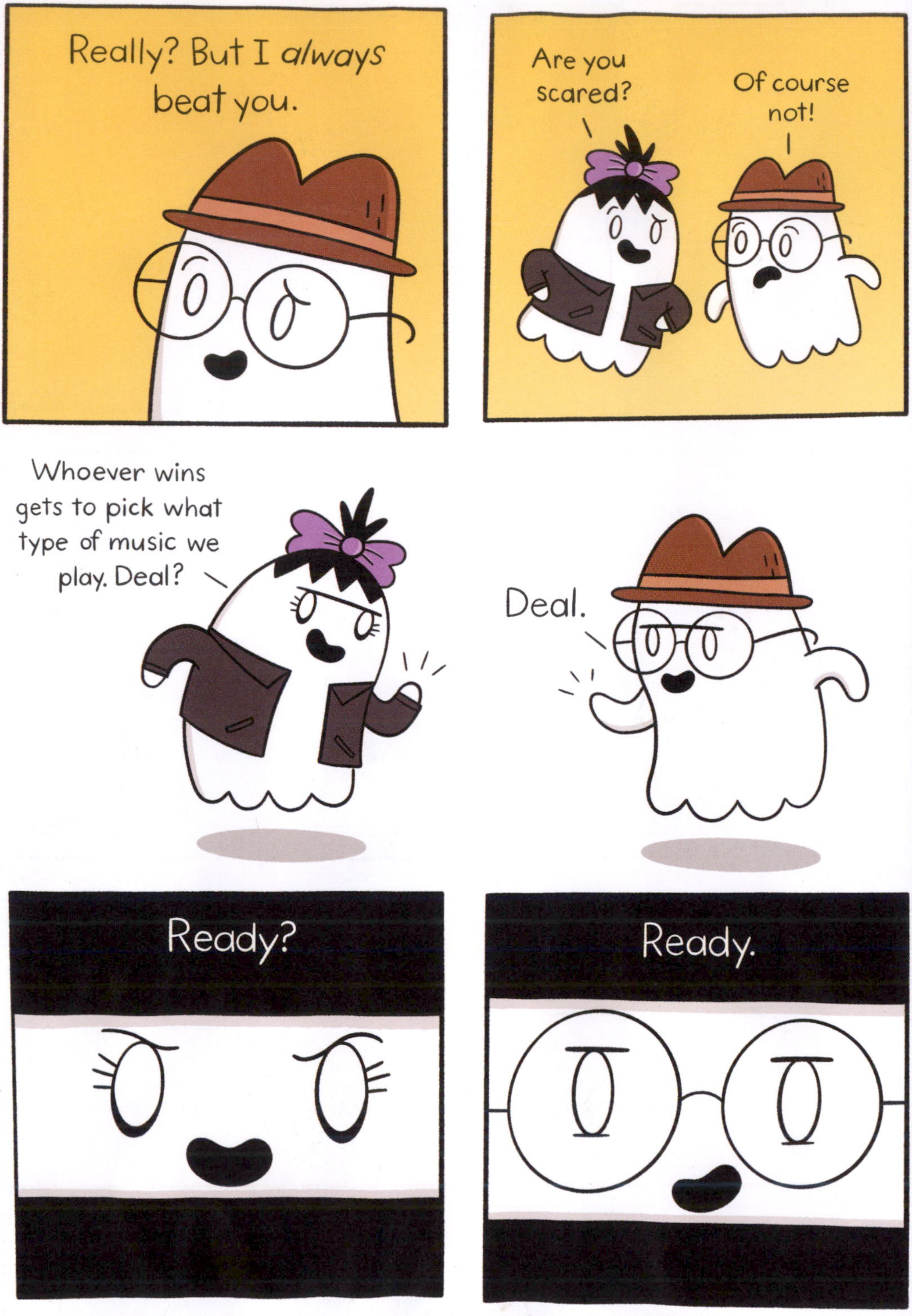
Really? But I *always* beat you.
Are you scared?
Of course not!
Whoever wins gets to pick what type of music we play. Deal?
Deal.
Ready?
Ready.

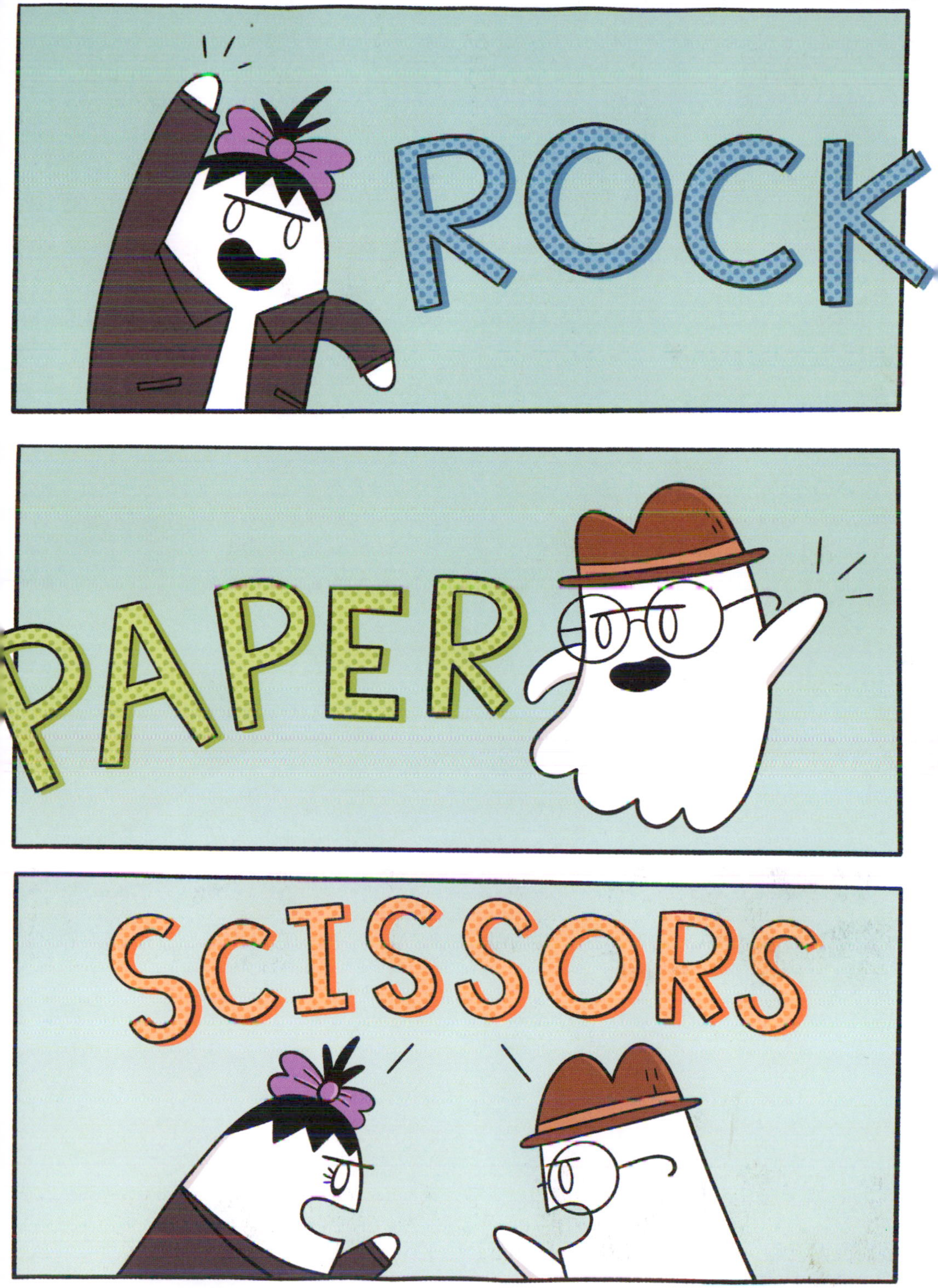
ROCK
PAPER
SCISSORS

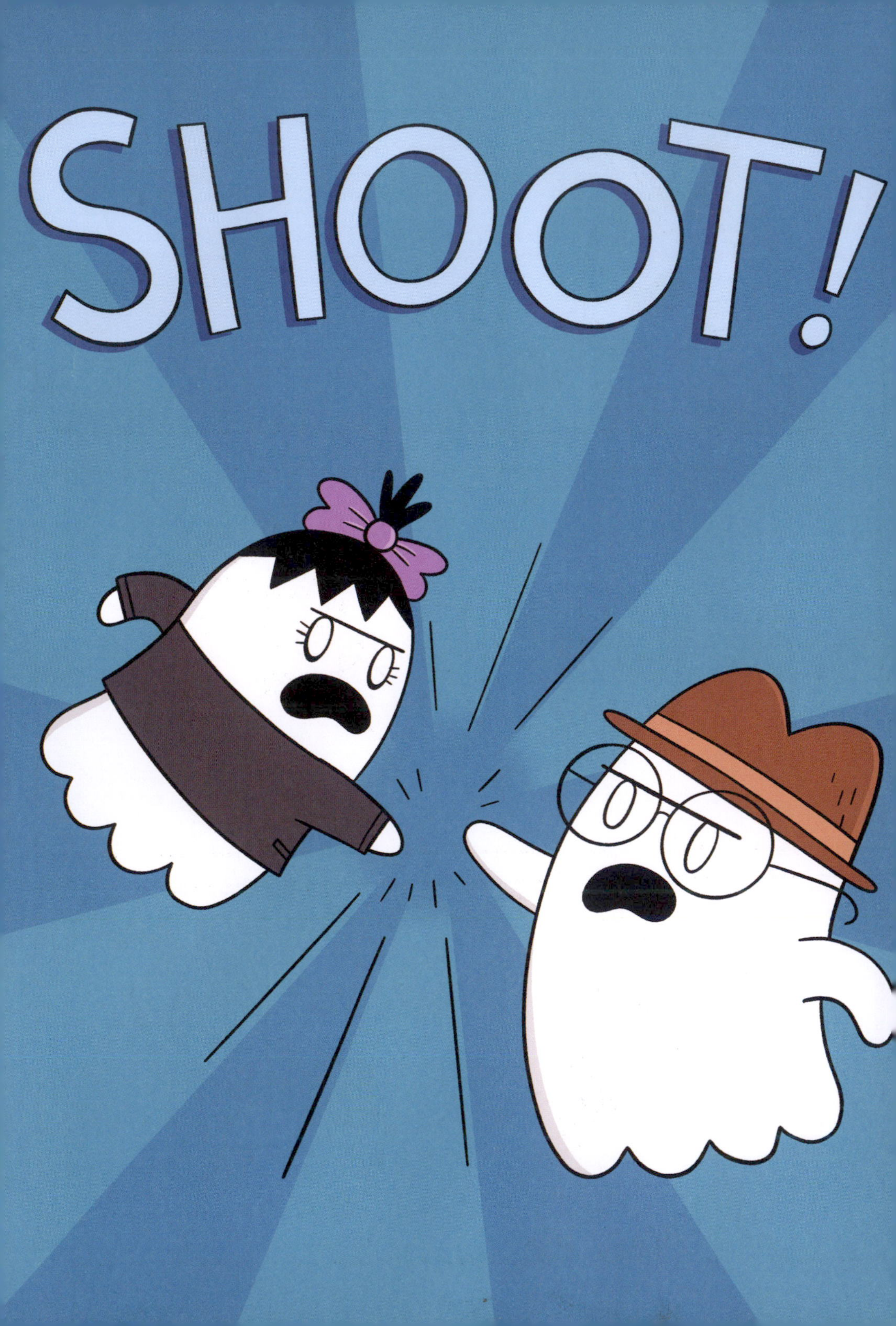
SHOOT!

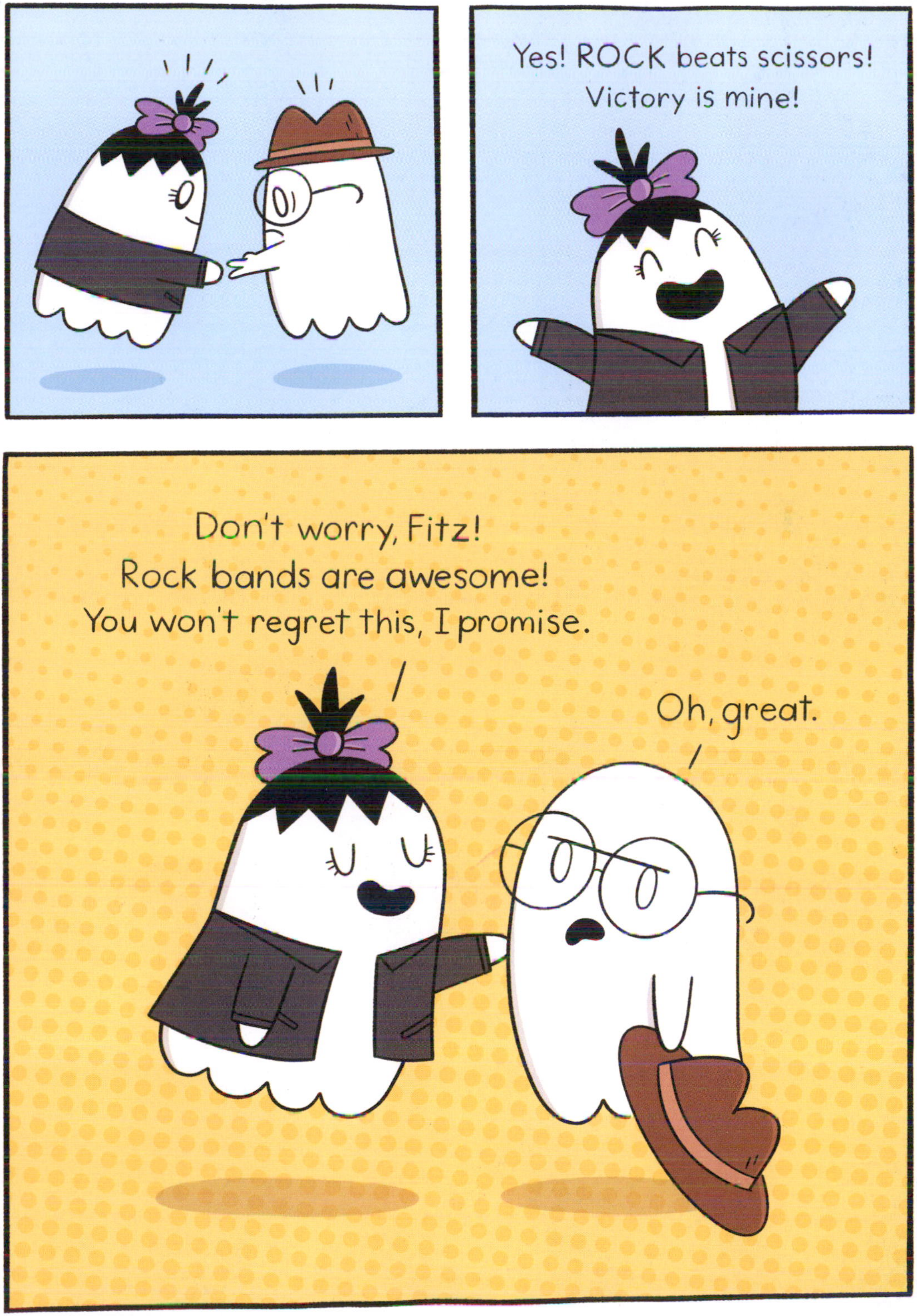
Yes! ROCK beats scissors! Victory is mine!
Don't worry, Fitz! Rock bands are awesome! You won't regret this, I promise.
Oh, great.

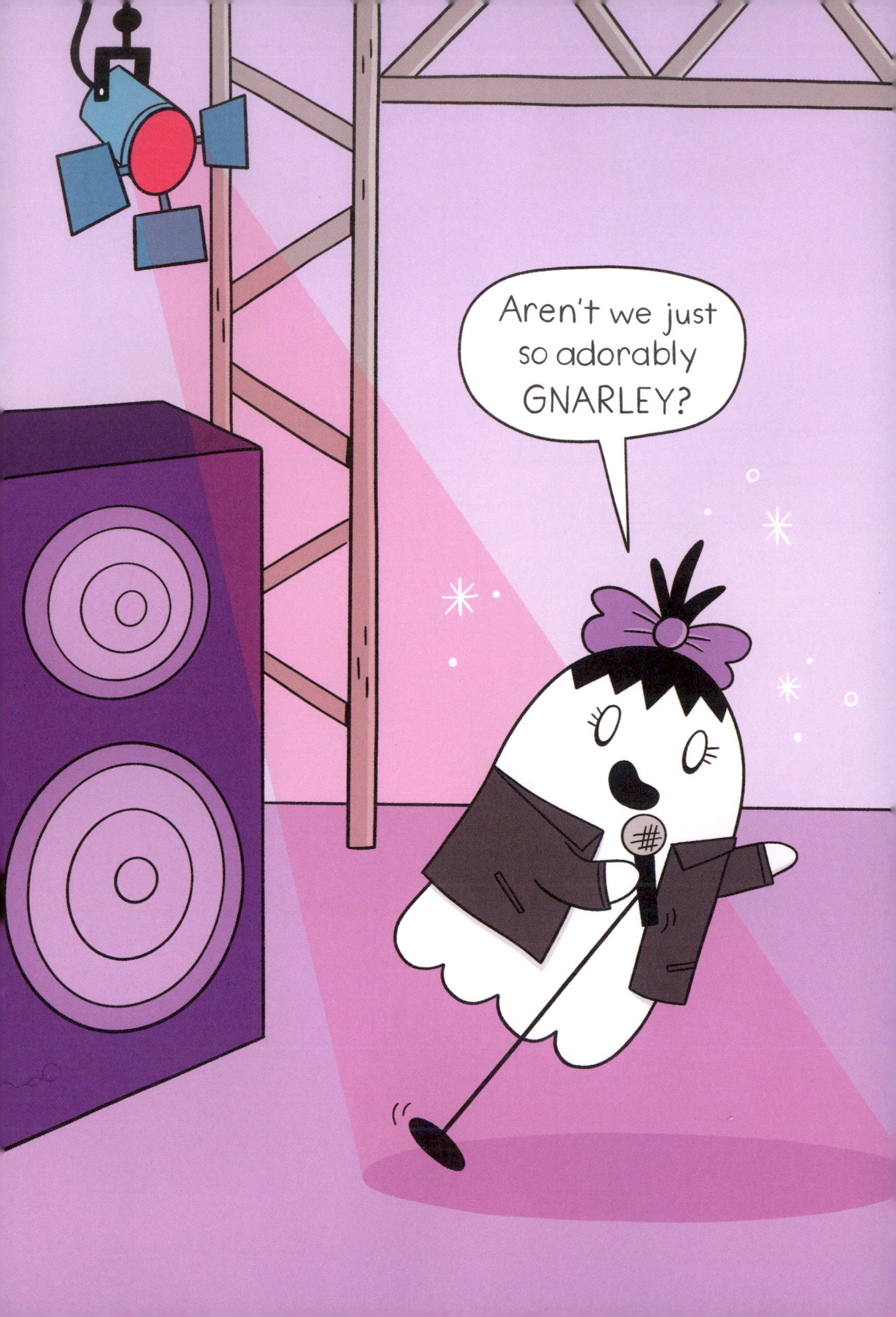
Aren't we just so adorably GNARLEY?

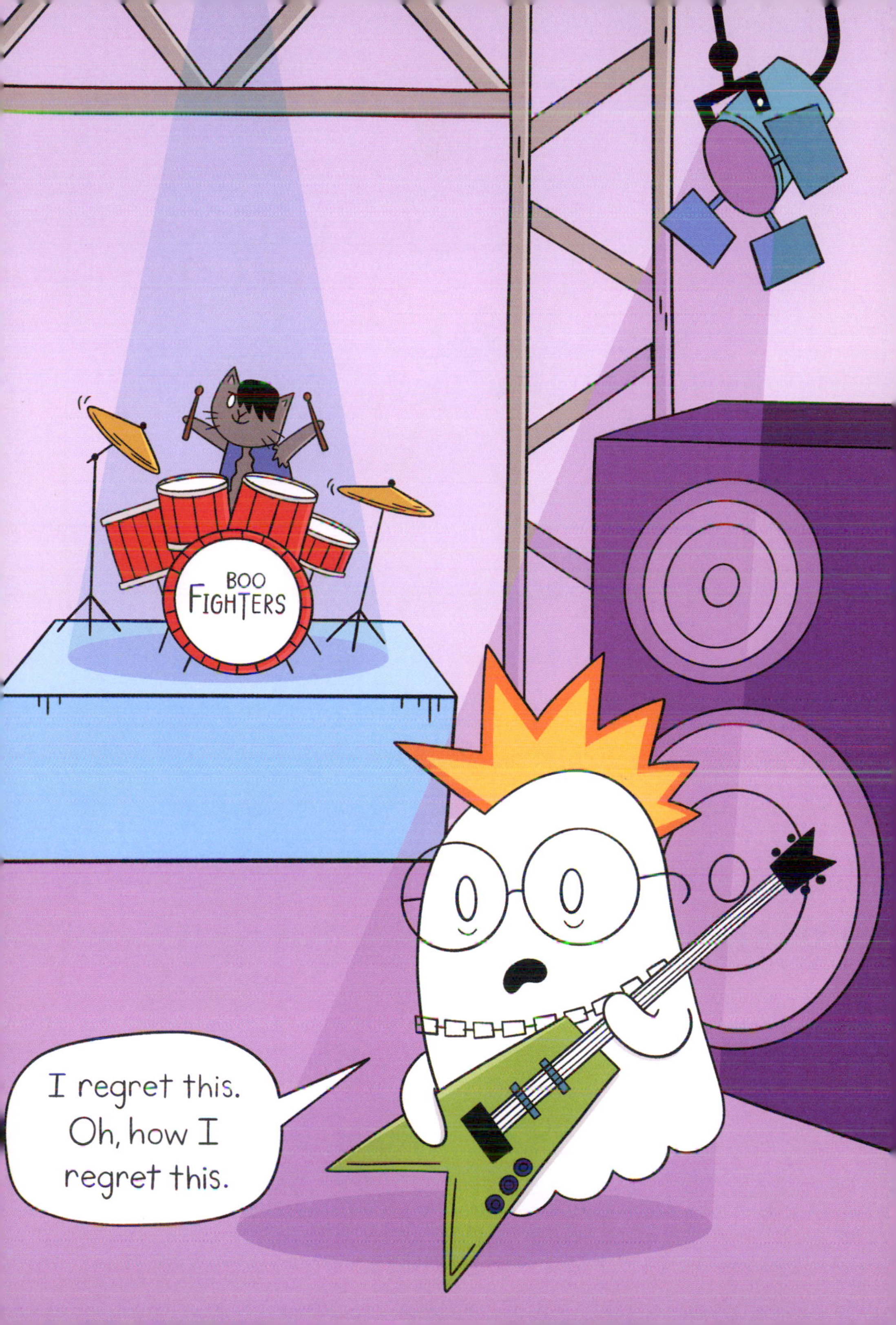
BOO FIGHTERS
I regret this. Oh, how I regret this.

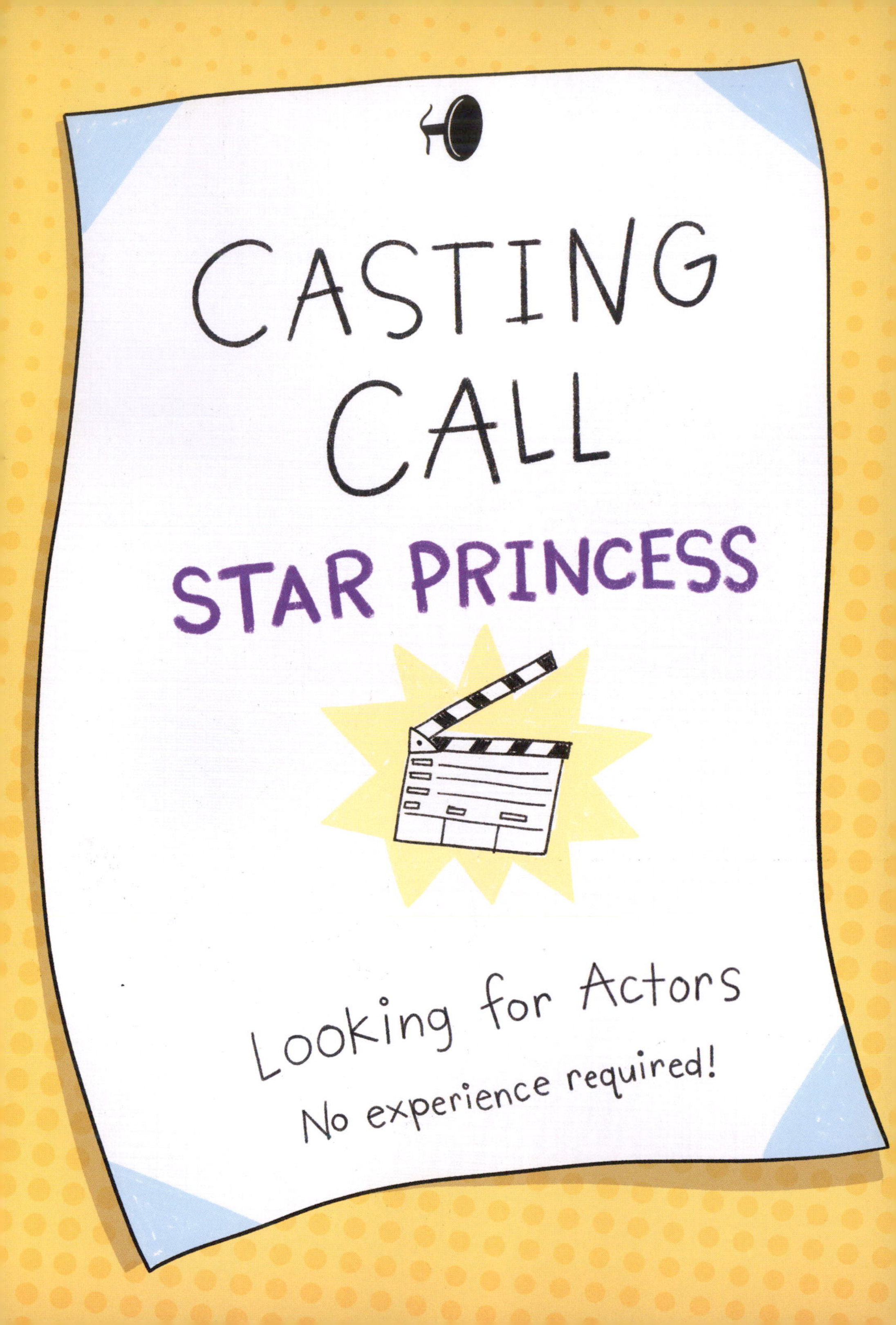

CASTING CALL
STAR PRINCESS
Looking for Actors
No experience required!

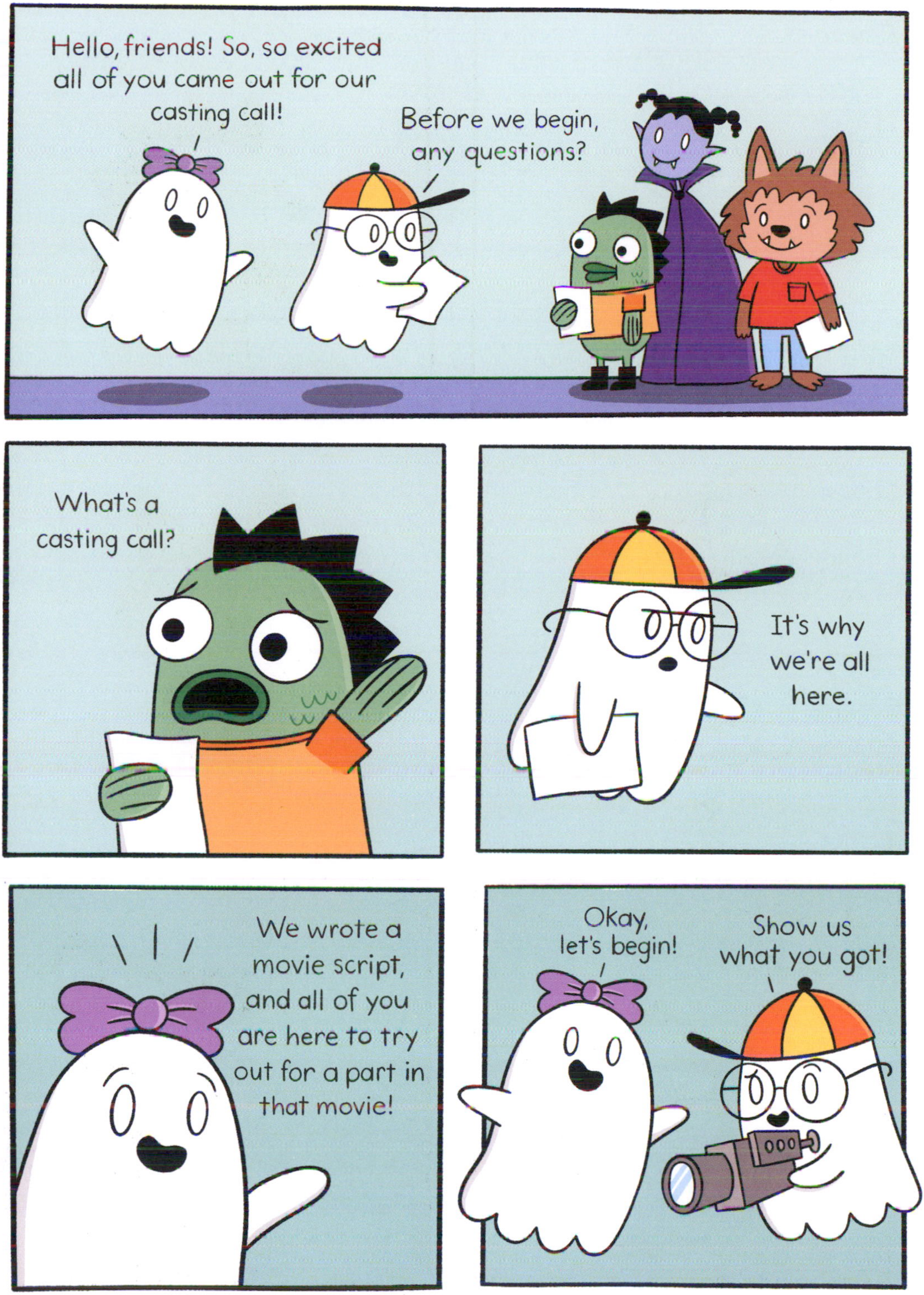
Hello, friends! So, so excited all of you came out for our casting call!
Before we begin, any questions?
What's a casting call?
It's why we're all here.
We wrote a movie script, and all of you are here to try out for a part in that movie!
Okay, let's begin!
Show us what you got!

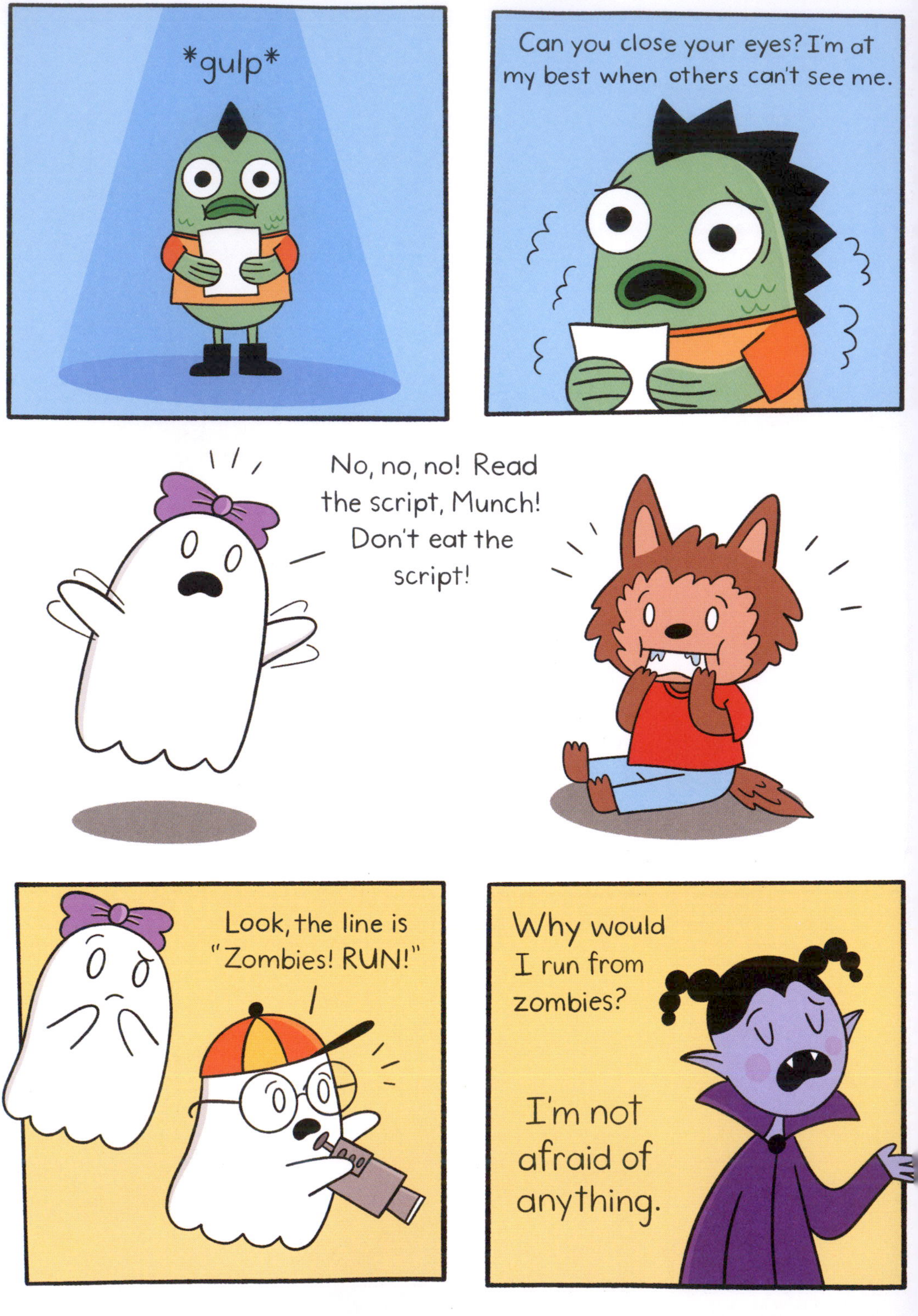
gulp
Can you close your eyes? I'm at my best when others can't see me.
No, no, no! Read the script, Munch! Don't eat the script!
Look, the line is "Zombies! RUN!"
Why would I run from zombies?
I'm not afraid of anything.

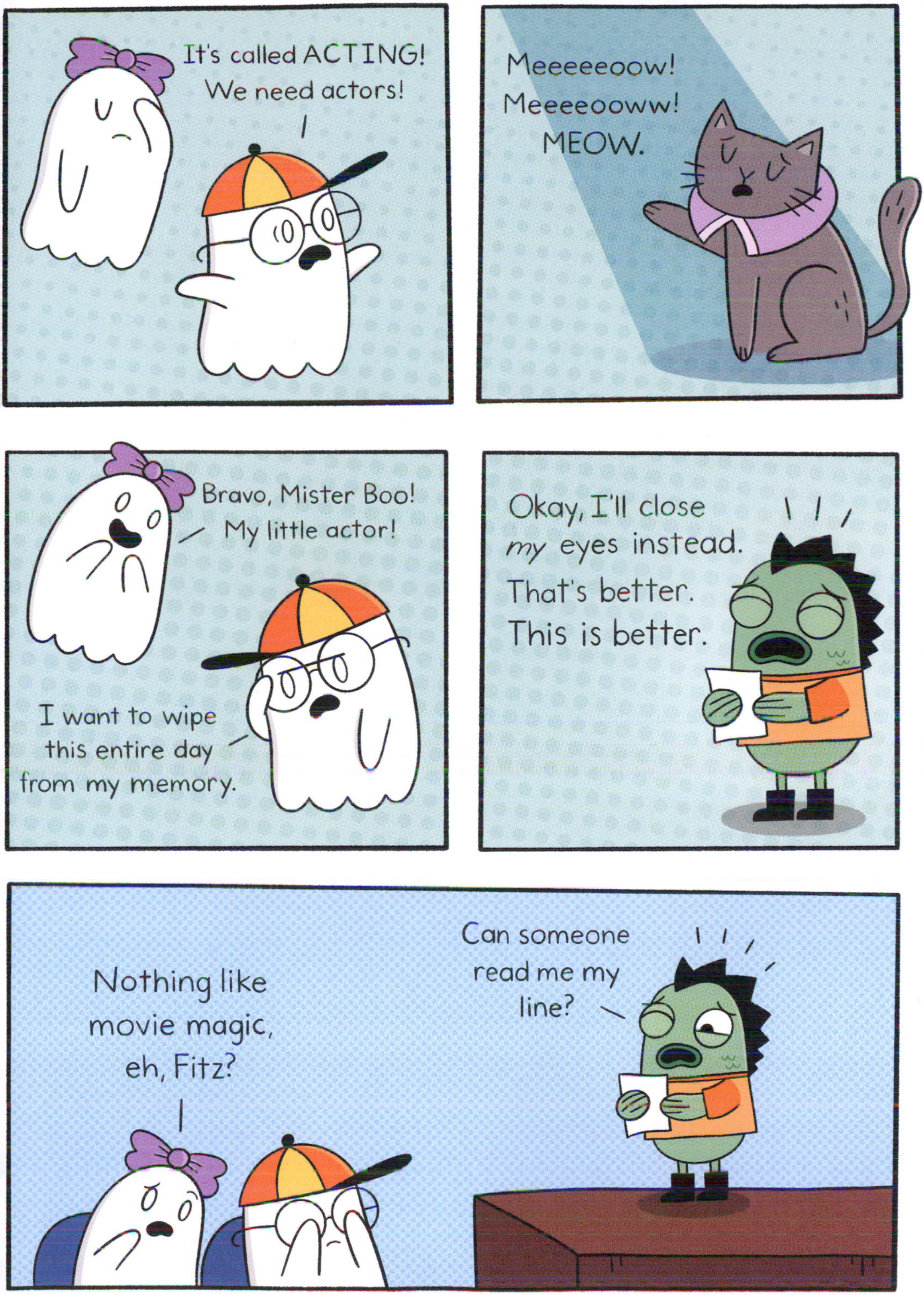
It's called ACTING! We need actors!
Meeeeeoow! Meeeeooww! MEOW.
Bravo, Mister Boo! My little actor!
I want to wipe this entire day from my memory.
Okay, I'll close *my* eyes instead. That's better. This is better.
Nothing like movie magic, eh, Fitz?
Can someone read me my line?

Rain of Terror

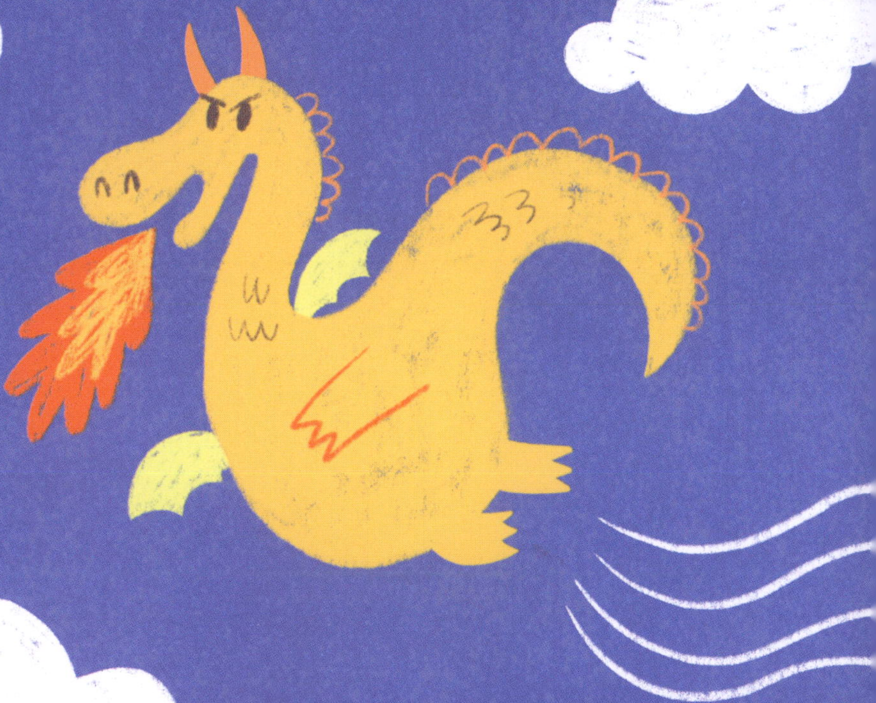

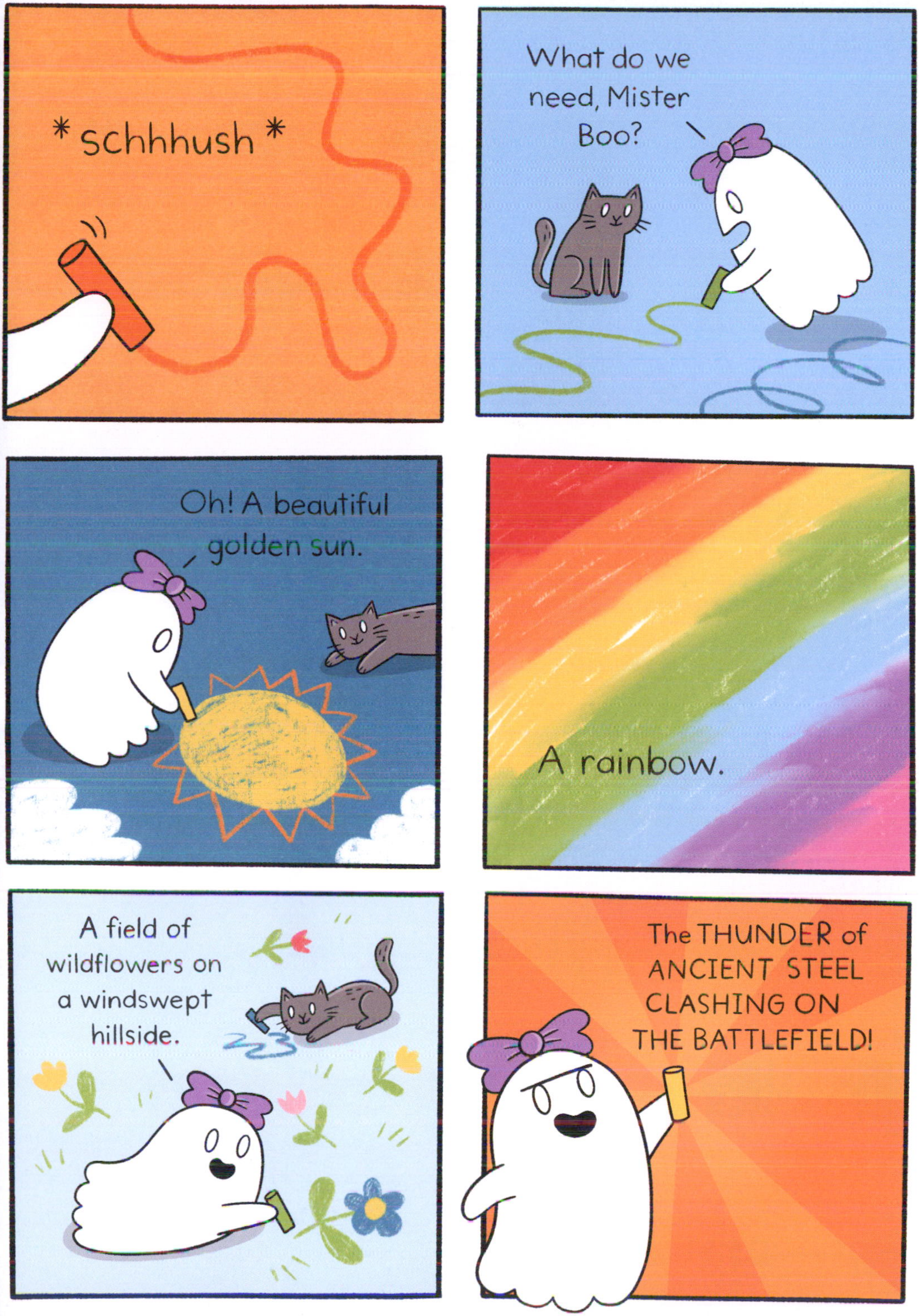
schhhush
What do we need, Mister Boo?
Oh! A beautiful golden sun.
A rainbow.
A field of wildflowers on a windswept hillside.
The THUNDER of ANCIENT STEEL CLASHING ON THE BATTLEFIELD!

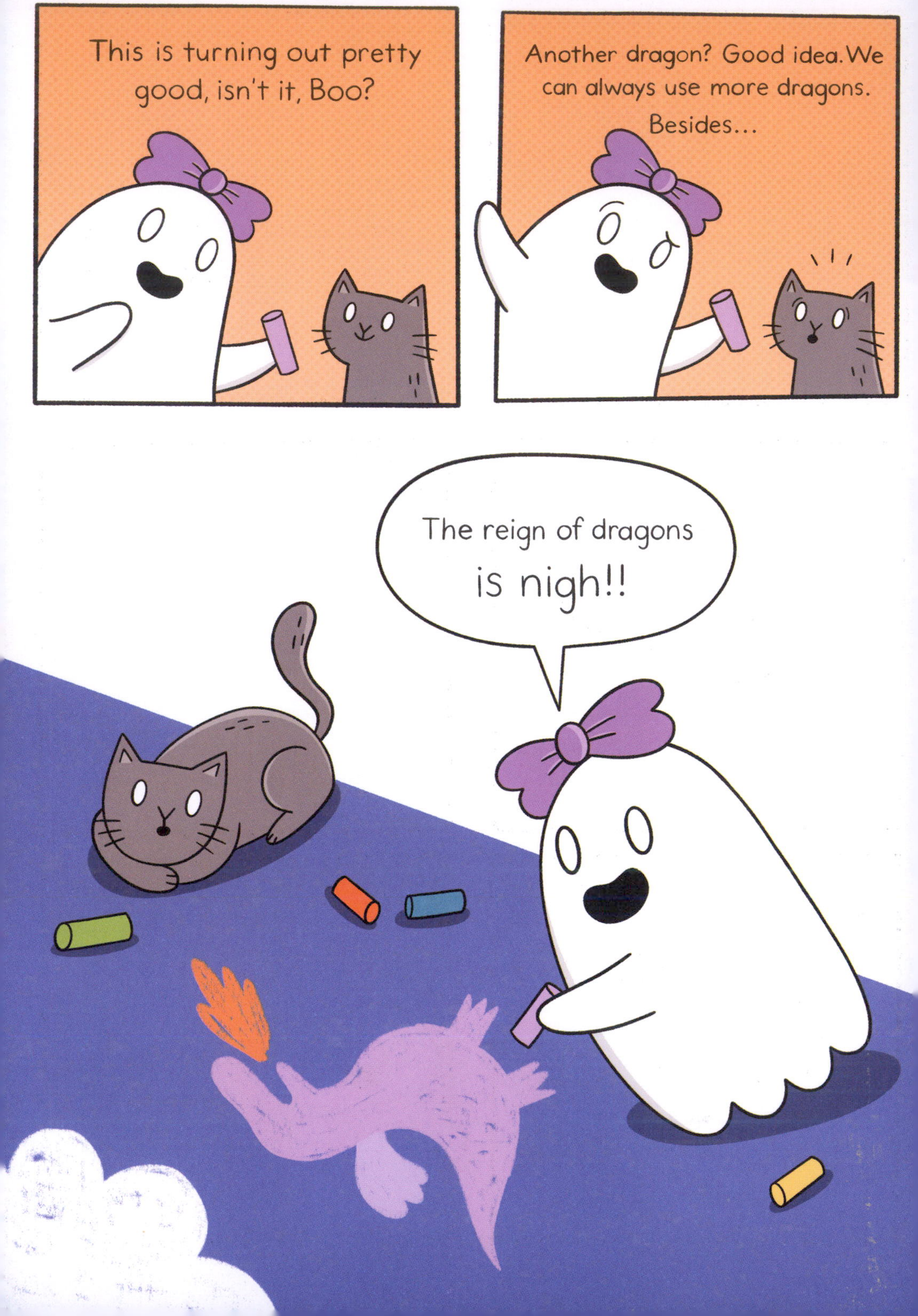
This is turning out pretty good, isn't it, Boo?
Another dragon? Good idea. We can always use more dragons. Besides...
The reign of dragons is nigh!!

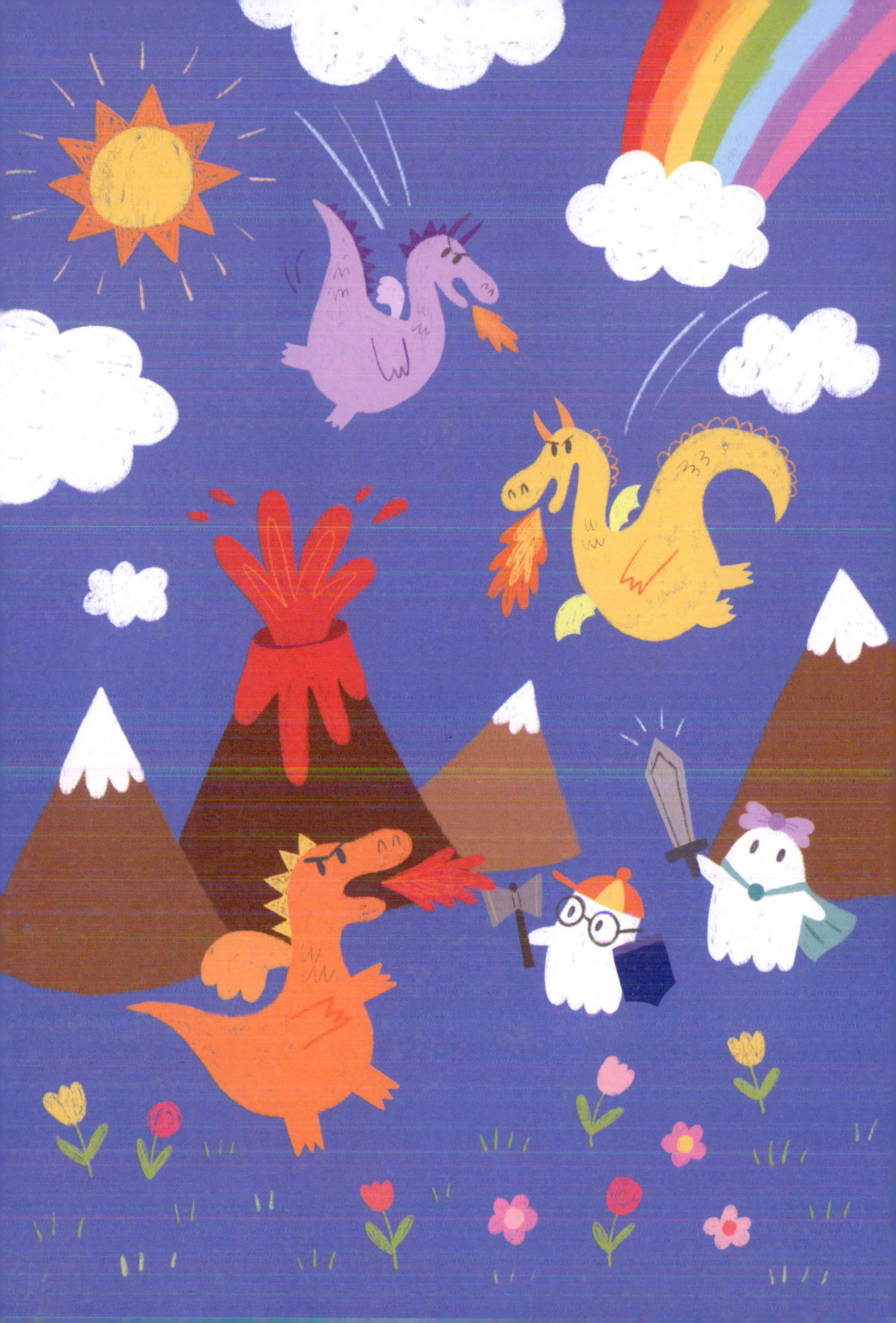

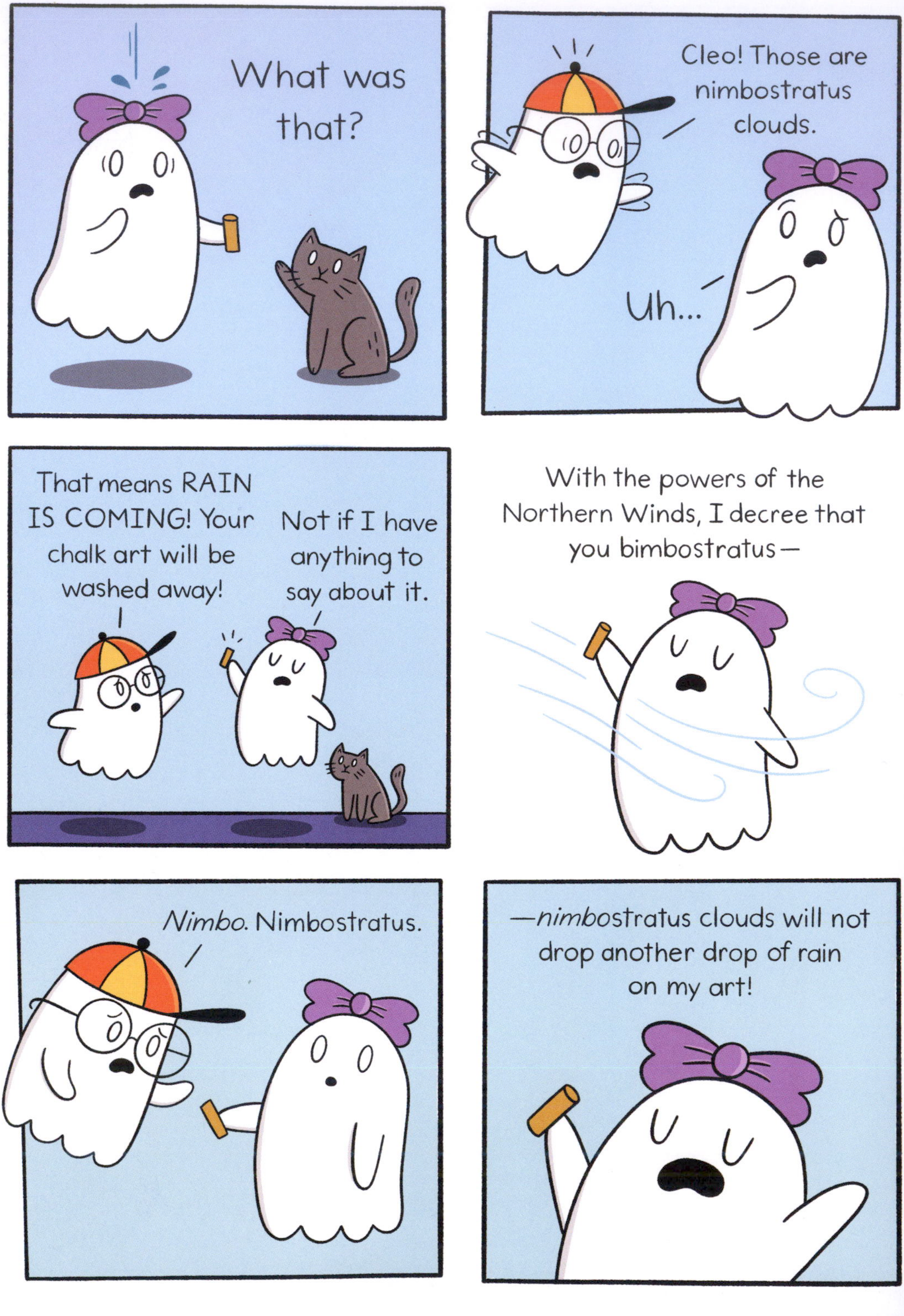
What was that?
Cleo! Those are nimbostratus clouds.
Uh...
That means RAIN IS COMING! Your chalk art will be washed away!
Not if I have anything to say about it.
With the powers of the Northern Winds, I decree that you bimbostratus—
Nimbo. Nimbostratus.
—*nimbo*stratus clouds will not drop another drop of rain on my art!

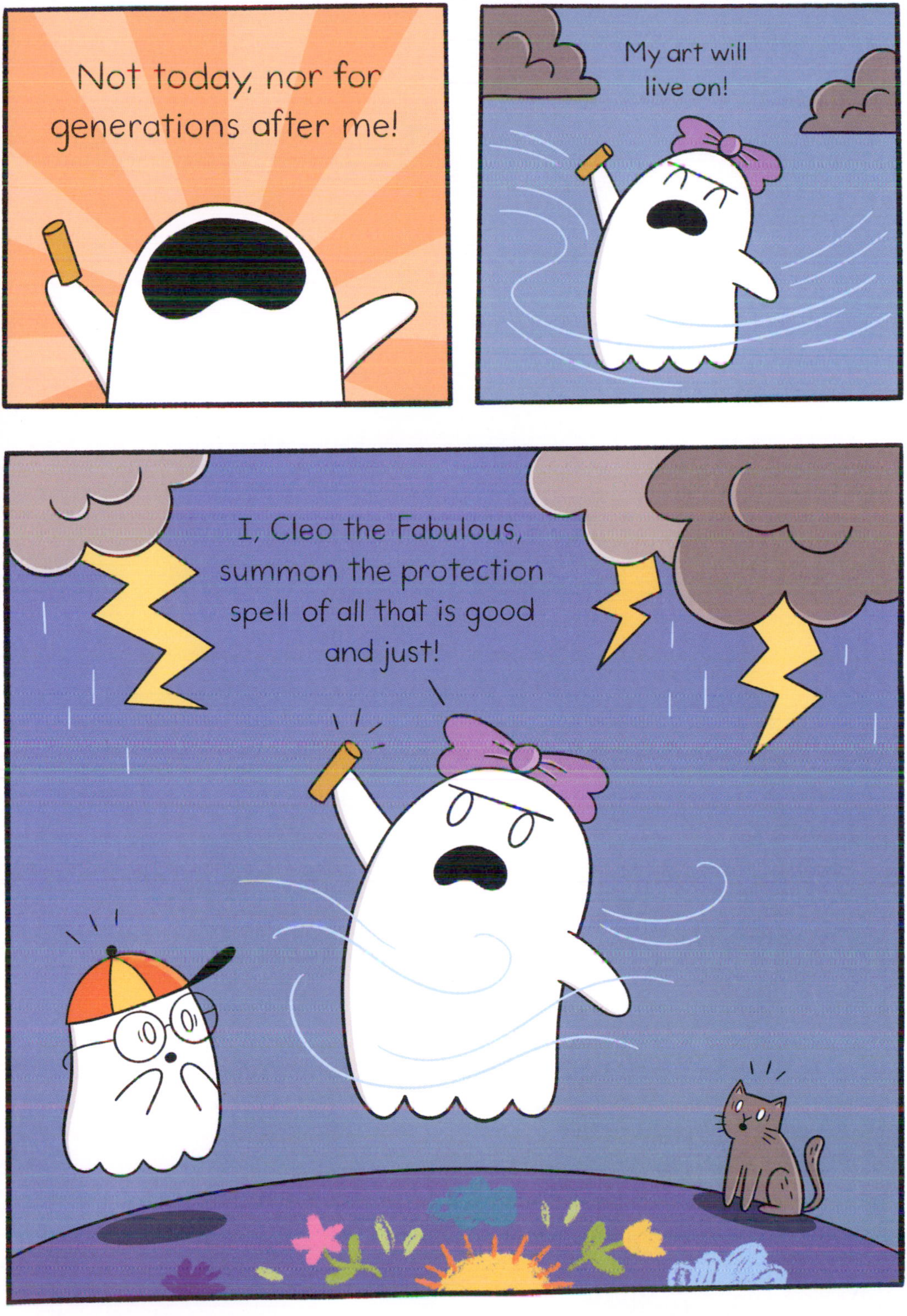
Not today, nor for generations after me!
My art will live on!
I, Cleo the Fabulous, summon the protection spell of all that is good and just!

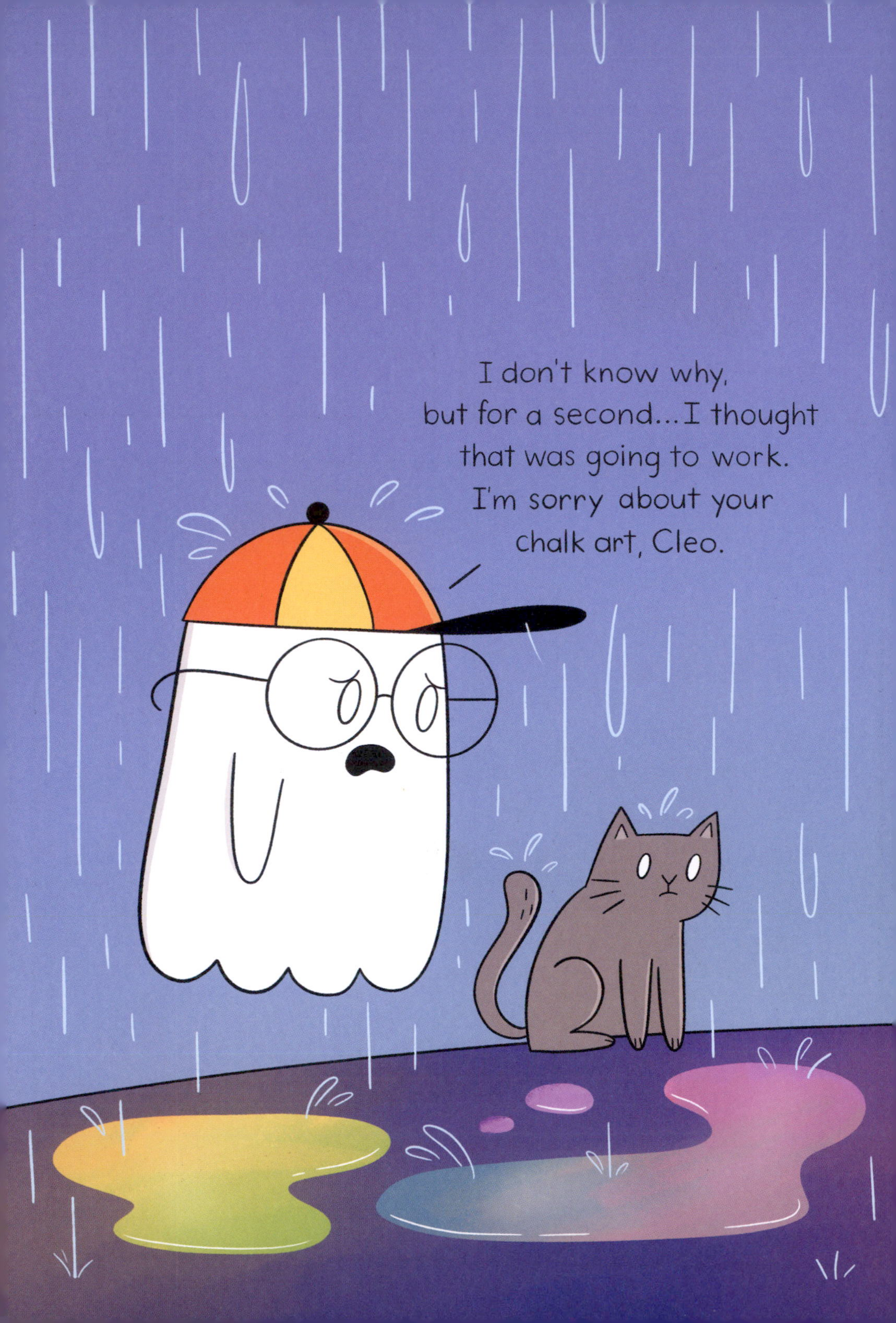
I don't know why, but for a second...I thought that was going to work. I'm sorry about your chalk art, Cleo.

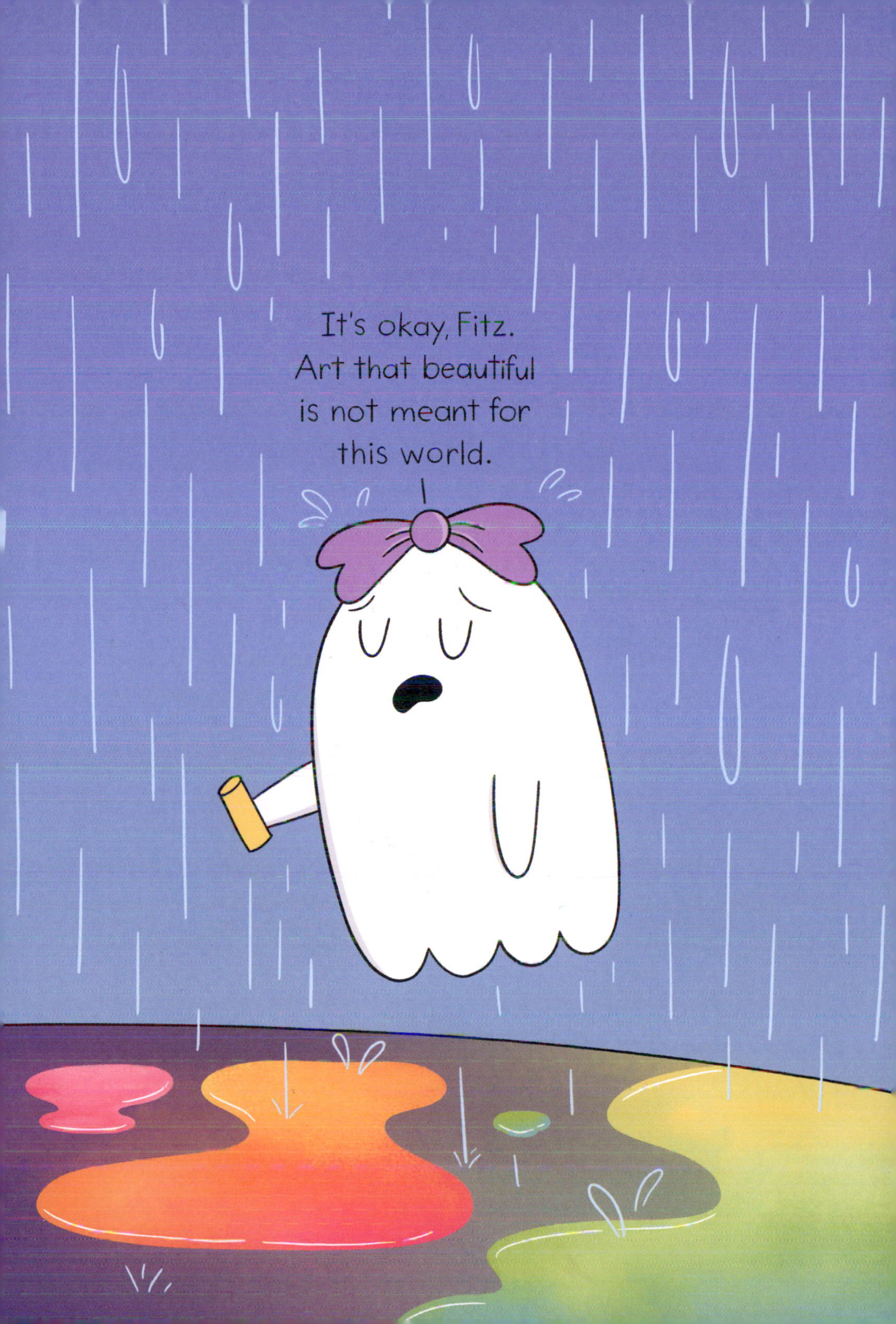
It's okay, Fitz.
Art that beautiful
is not meant for
this world.

The Rude Goldberg

PLANS

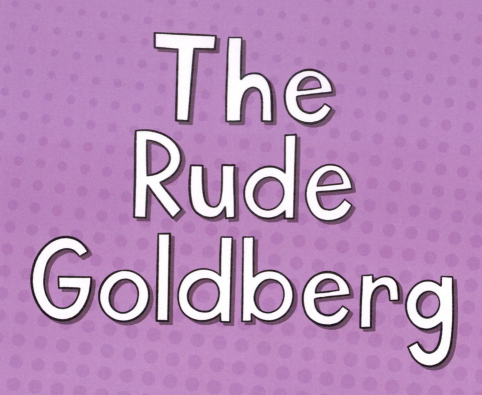

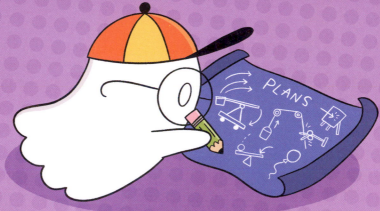

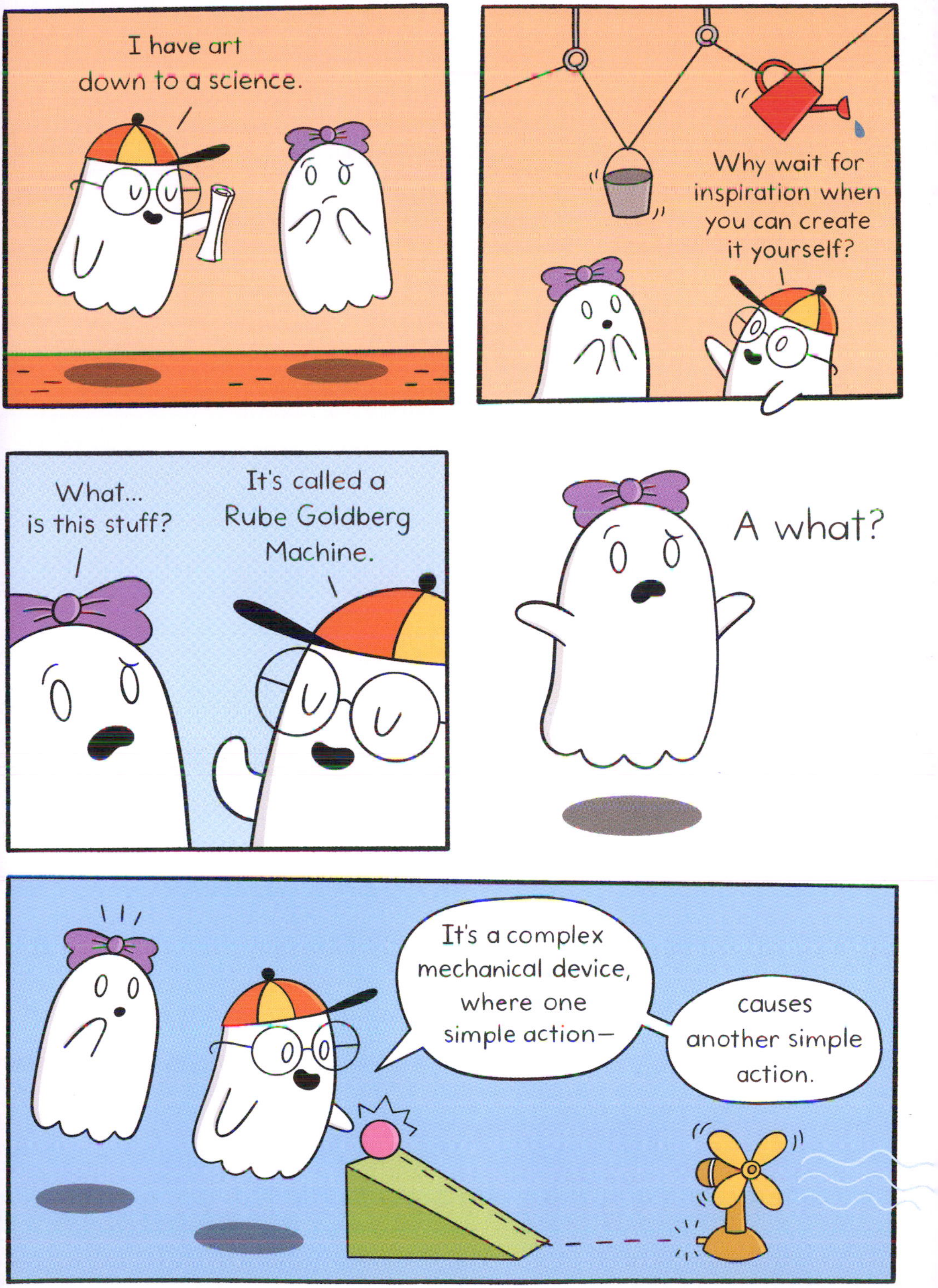
I have art down to a science.
Why wait for inspiration when you can create it yourself?
What... is this stuff?
It's called a Rube Goldberg Machine.
A what?
It's a complex mechanical device, where one simple action—
causes another simple action.

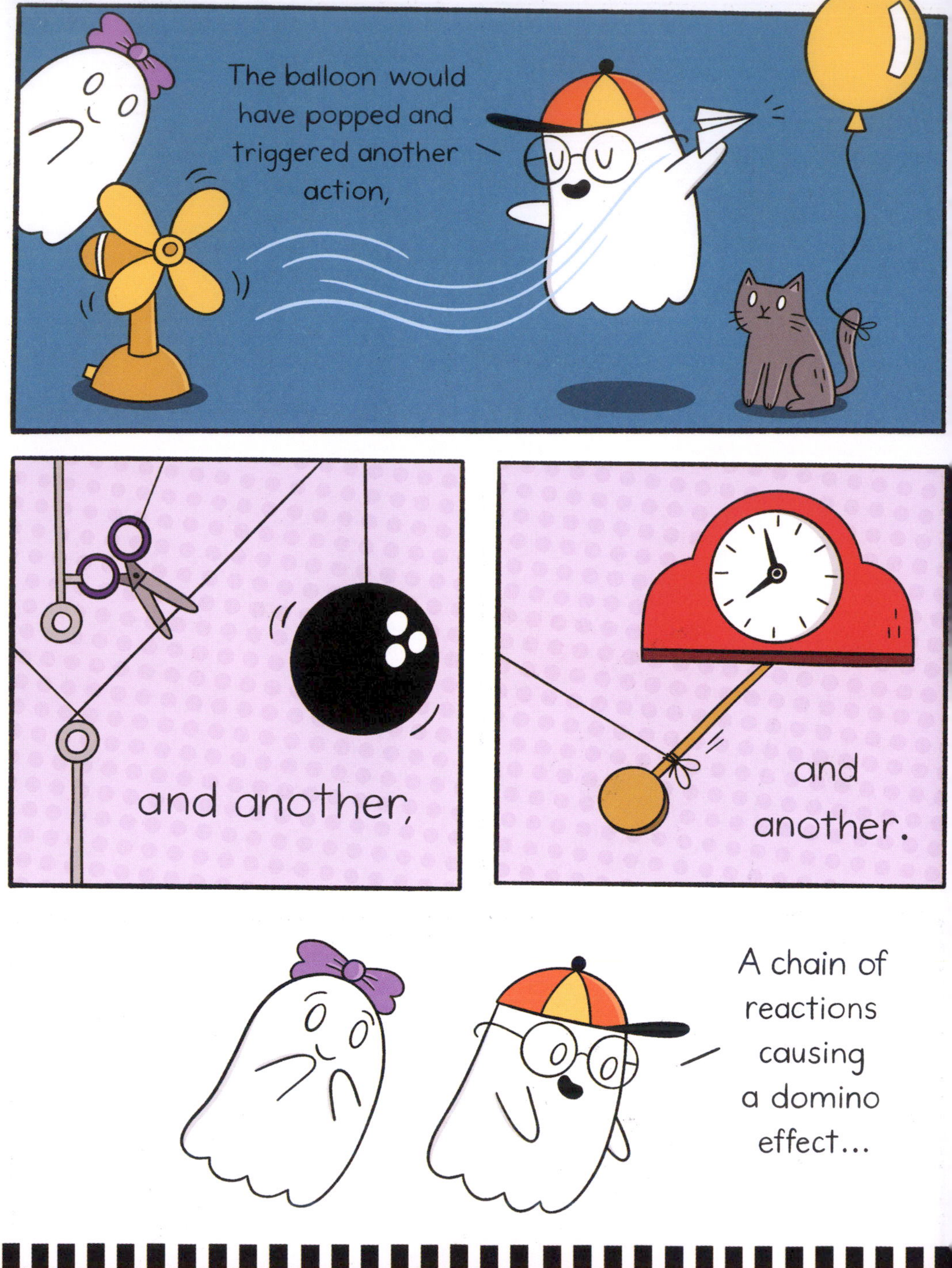

The balloon would have popped and triggered another action,
and another,
and another.
A chain of reactions causing a domino effect...

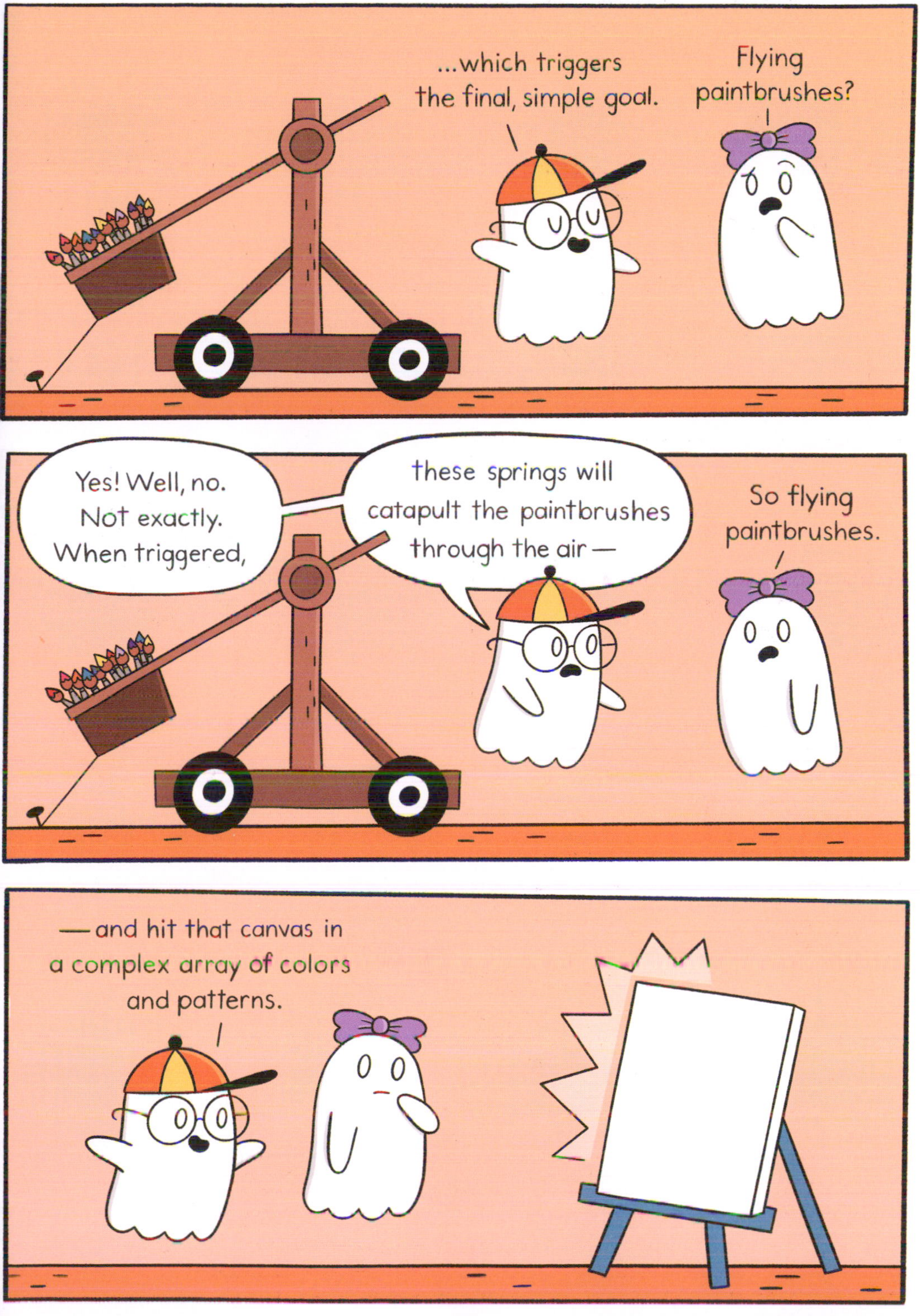
...which triggers the final, simple goal.
Flying paintbrushes?
Yes! Well, no. Not exactly. When triggered,
these springs will catapult the paintbrushes through the air—
So flying paintbrushes.
—and hit that canvas in a complex array of colors and patterns.

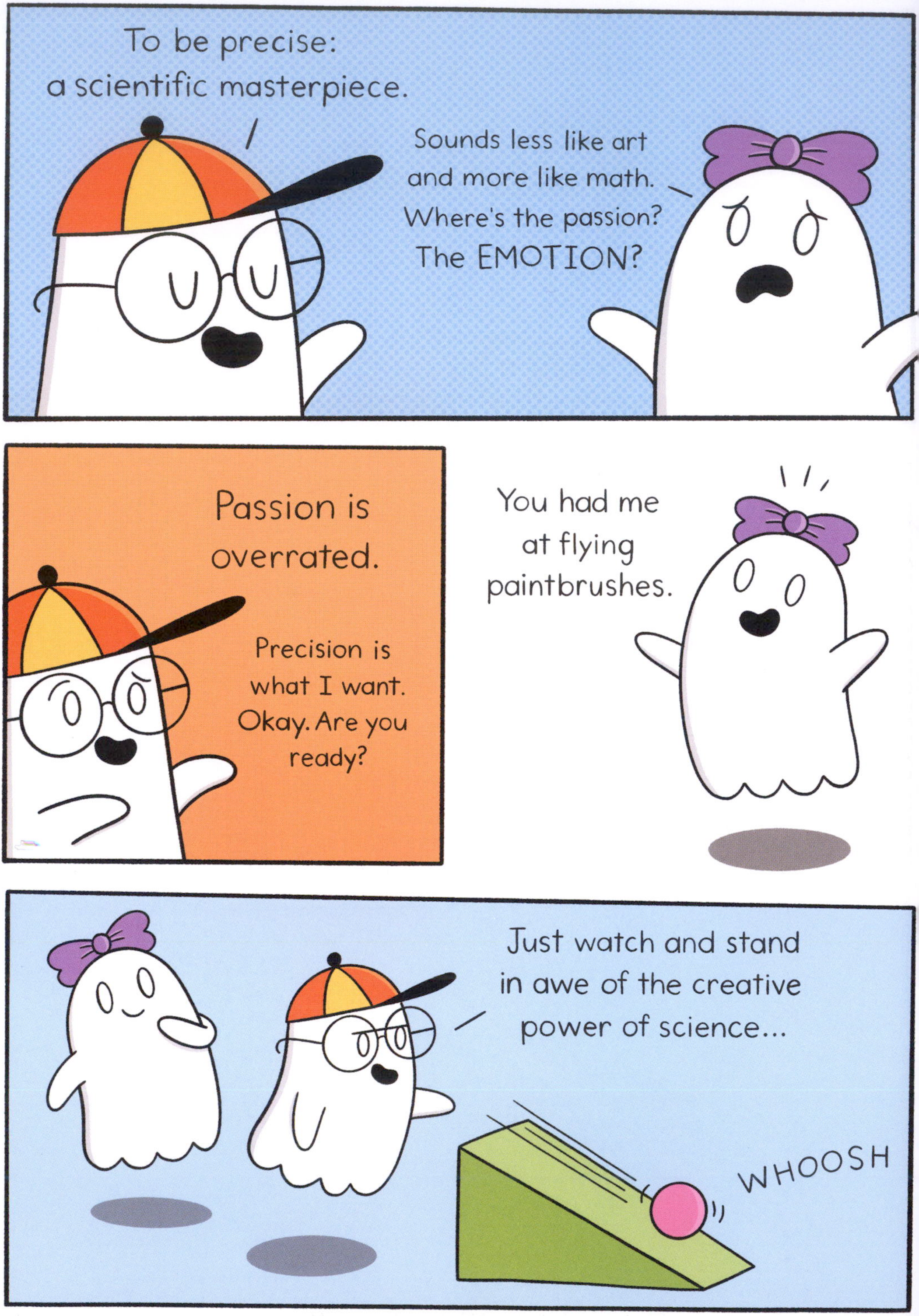
To be precise:
a scientific masterpiece.
Sounds less like art
and more like math.
Where's the passion?
The EMOTION?
Passion is
overrated.
Precision is
what I want.
Okay. Are you
ready?
You had me
at flying
paintbrushes.
Just watch and stand
in awe of the creative
power of science...
WHOOSH

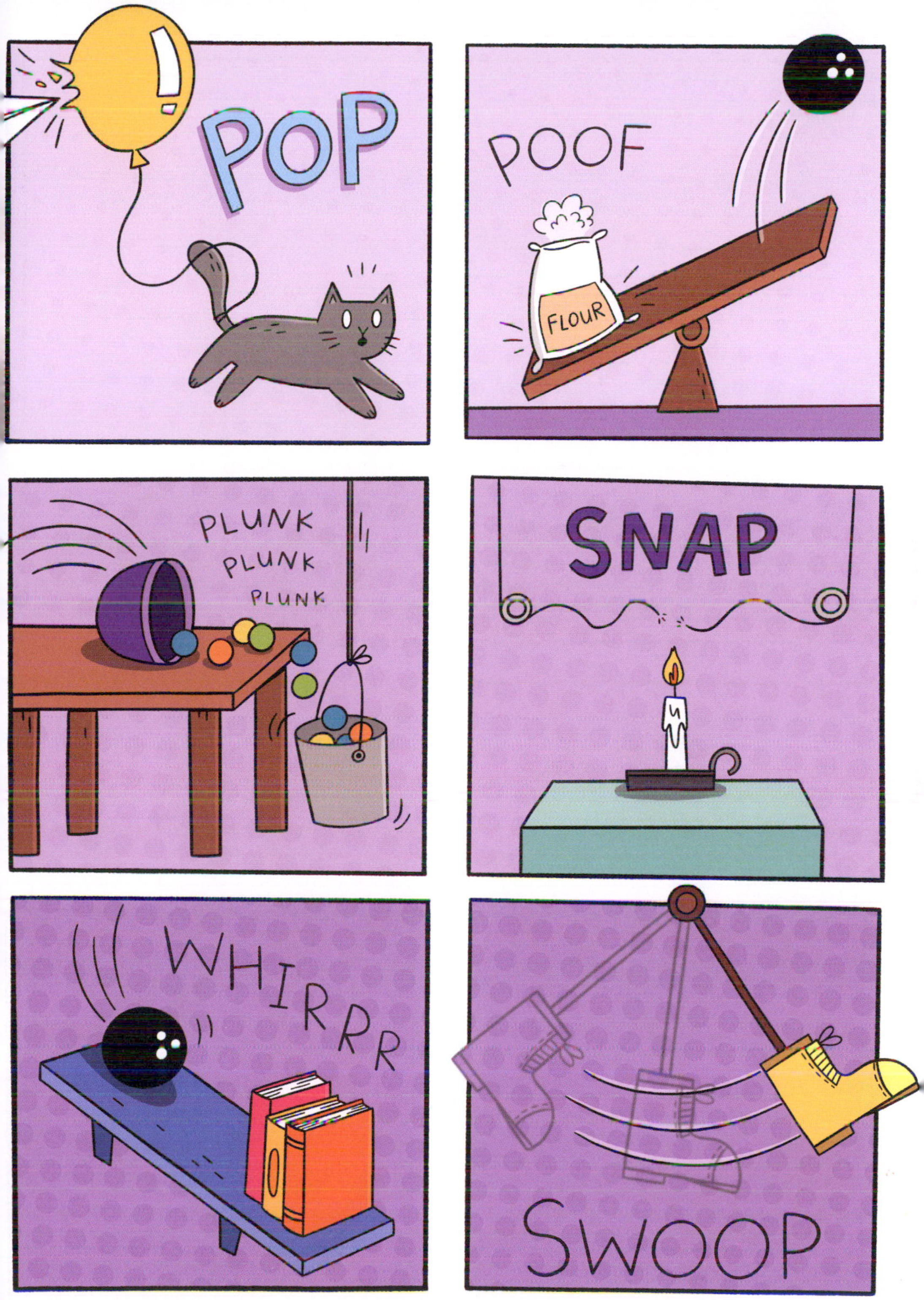
POP
POOF
FLOUR
PLUNK
PLUNK
PLUNK
SNAP
WHIRRR
SWOOP

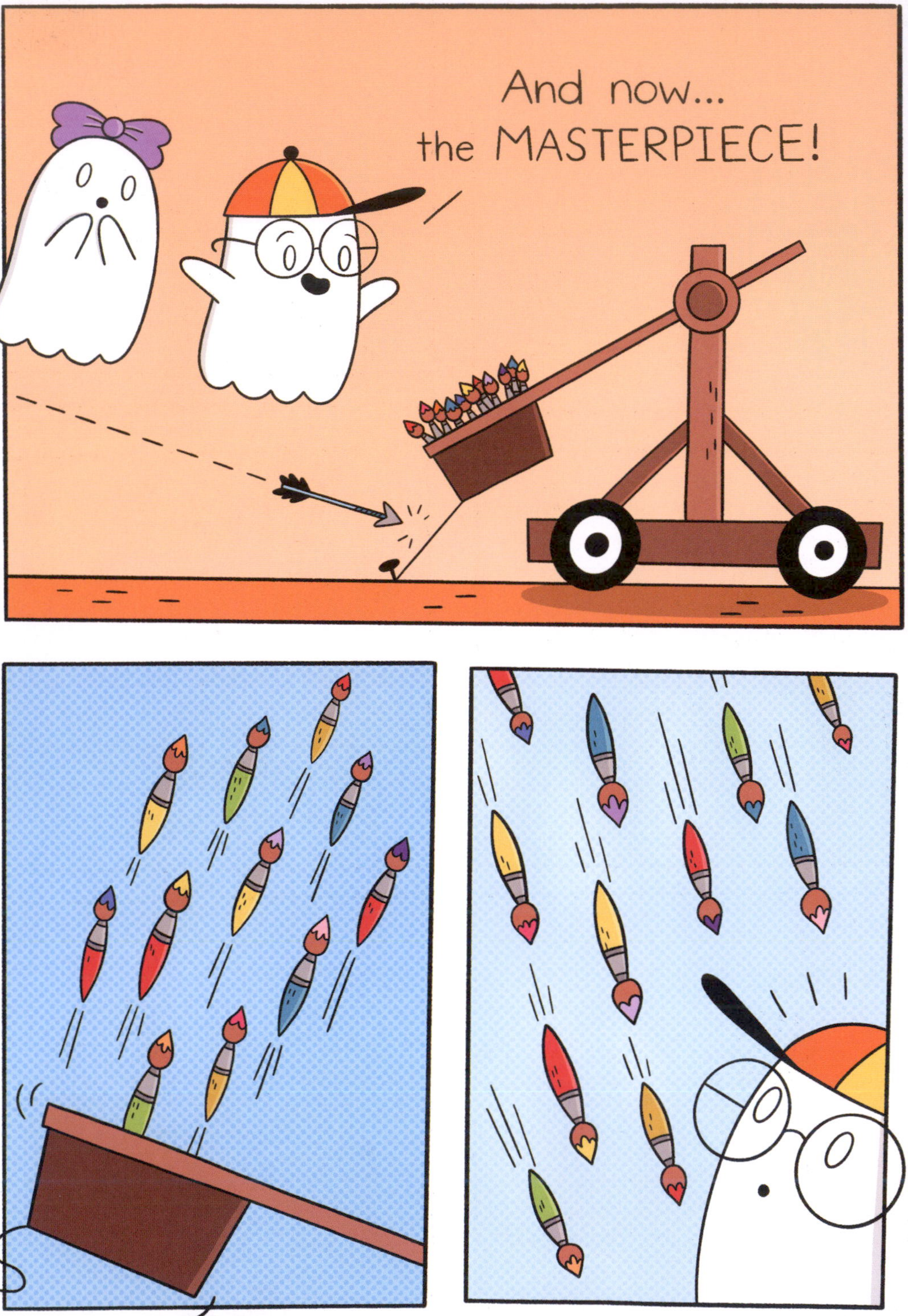
And now...
the MASTERPIECE!

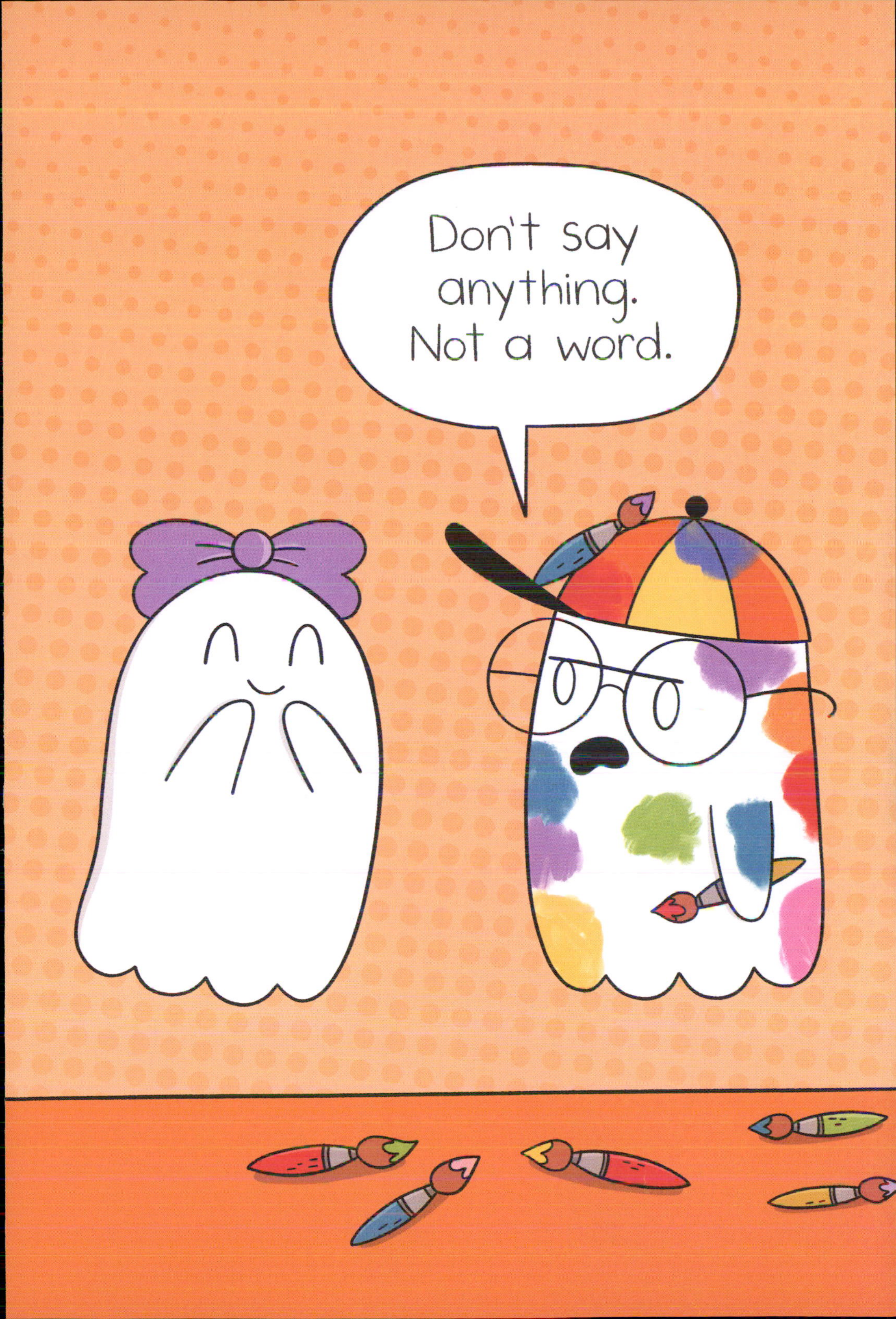
Don't say anything. Not a word.

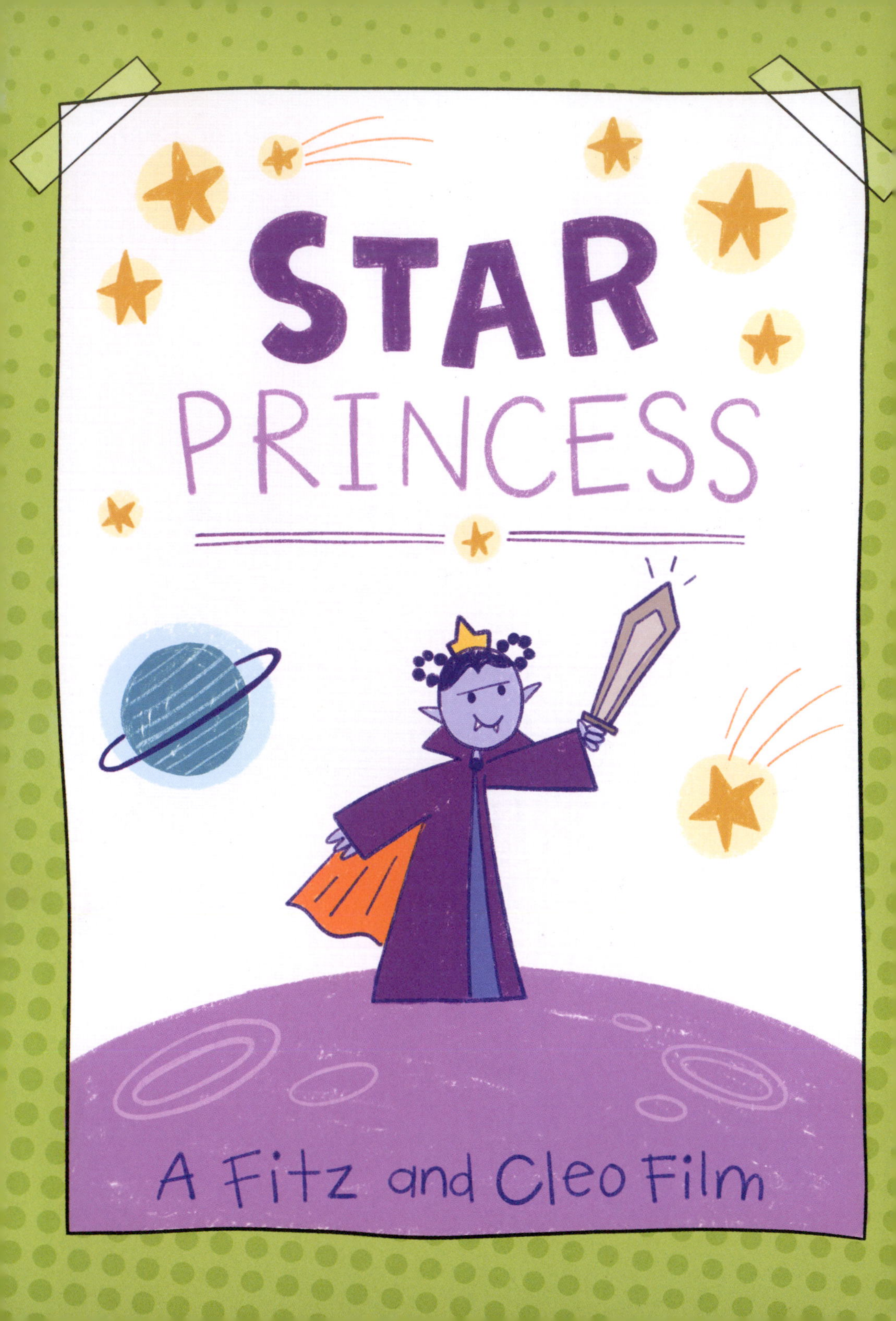
STAR
PRINCESS
A Fitz and Cleo Film

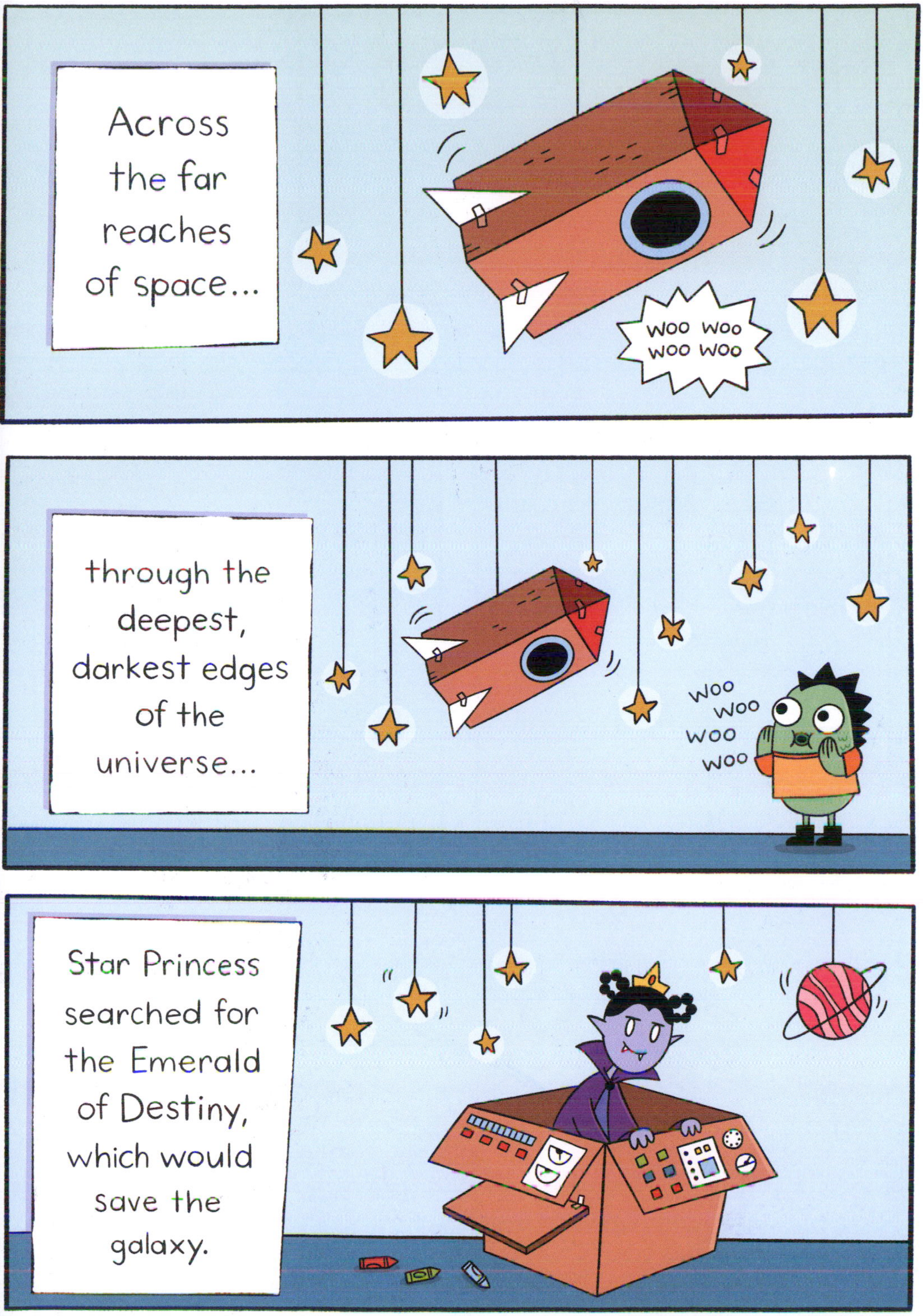
Across the far reaches of space...
WOO WOO WOO WOO
through the deepest, darkest edges of the universe...
WOO WOO WOO WOO
Star Princess searched for the Emerald of Destiny, which would save the galaxy.

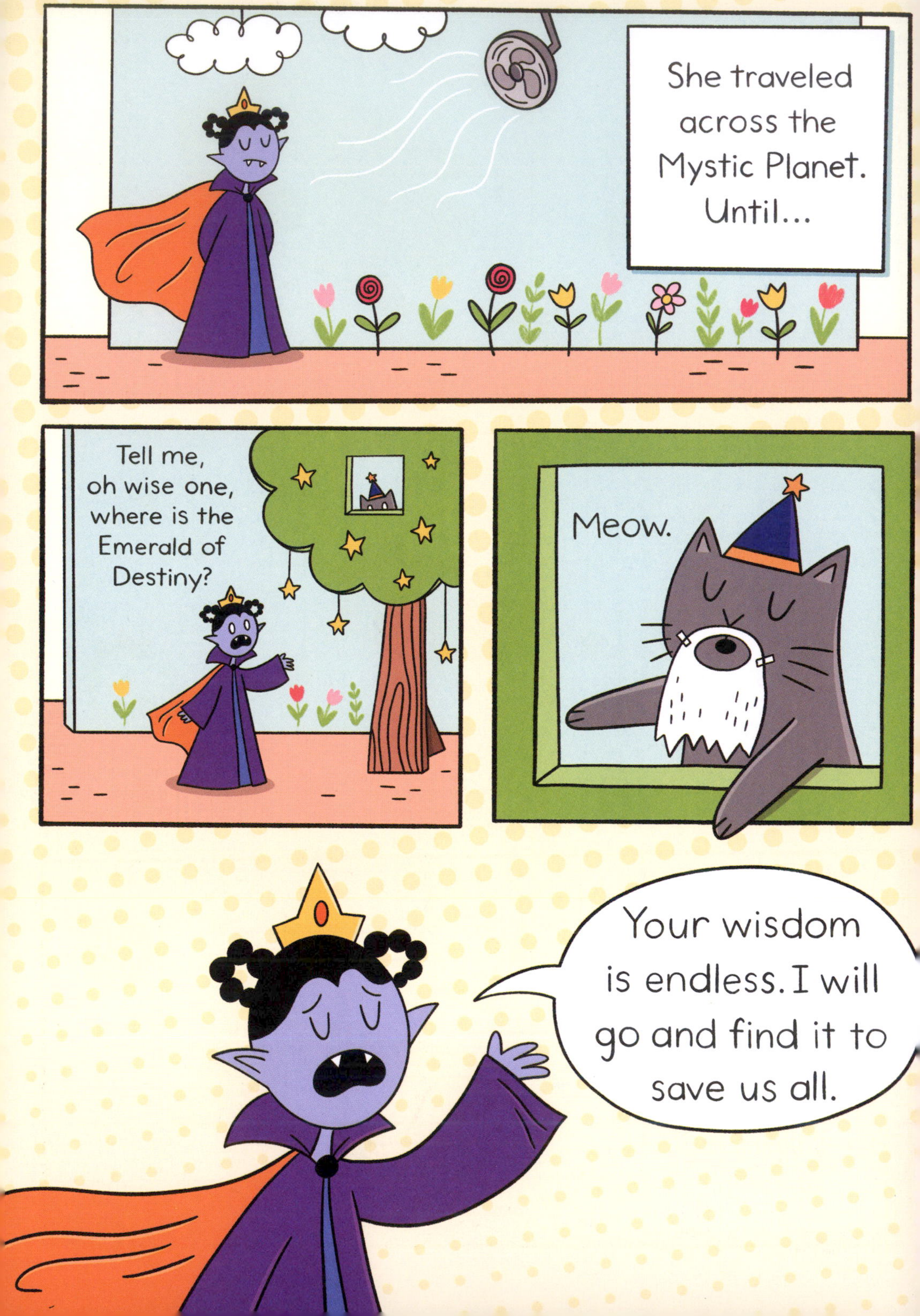

She traveled across the Mystic Planet. Until...
Tell me, oh wise one, where is the Emerald of Destiny?
Meow.
Your wisdom is endless. I will go and find it to save us all.

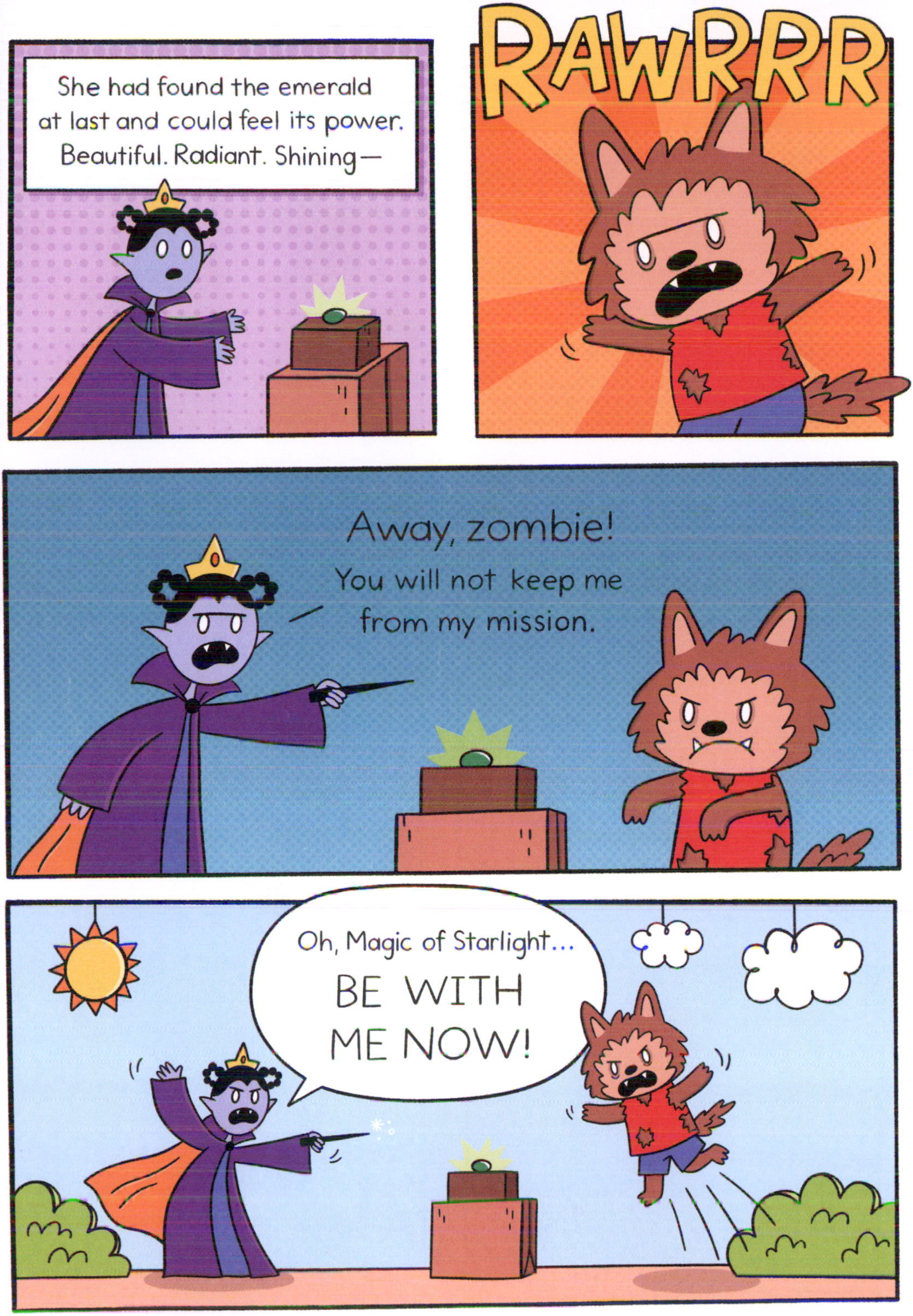
She had found the emerald at last and could feel its power. Beautiful. Radiant. Shining—
RAWRRR
Away, zombie!
You will not keep me from my mission.
Oh, Magic of Starlight...
BE WITH ME NOW!

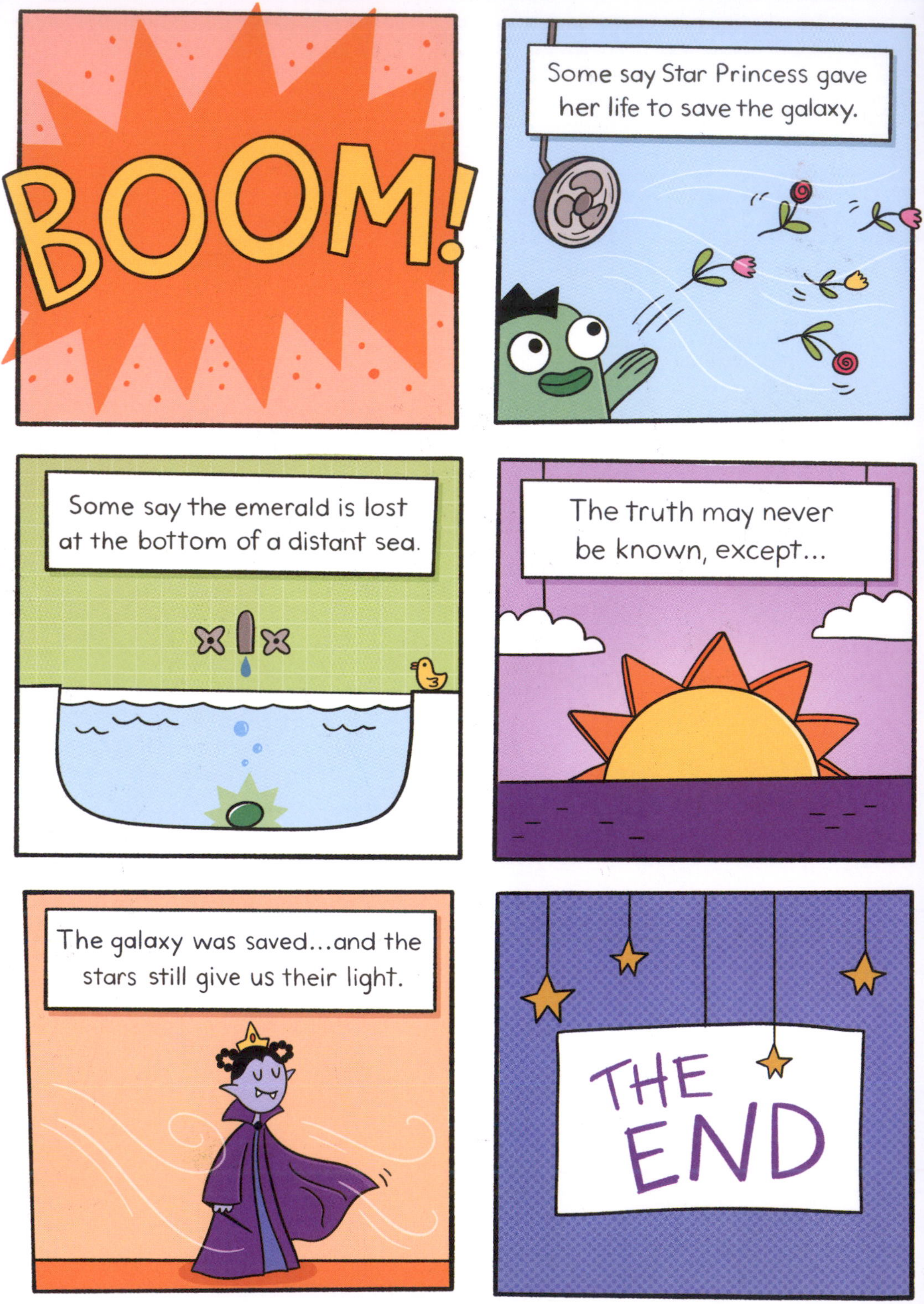
BOOM!
Some say Star Princess gave her life to save the galaxy.
Some say the emerald is lost at the bottom of a distant sea.
The truth may never be known, except...
The galaxy was saved...and the stars still give us their light.
THE END

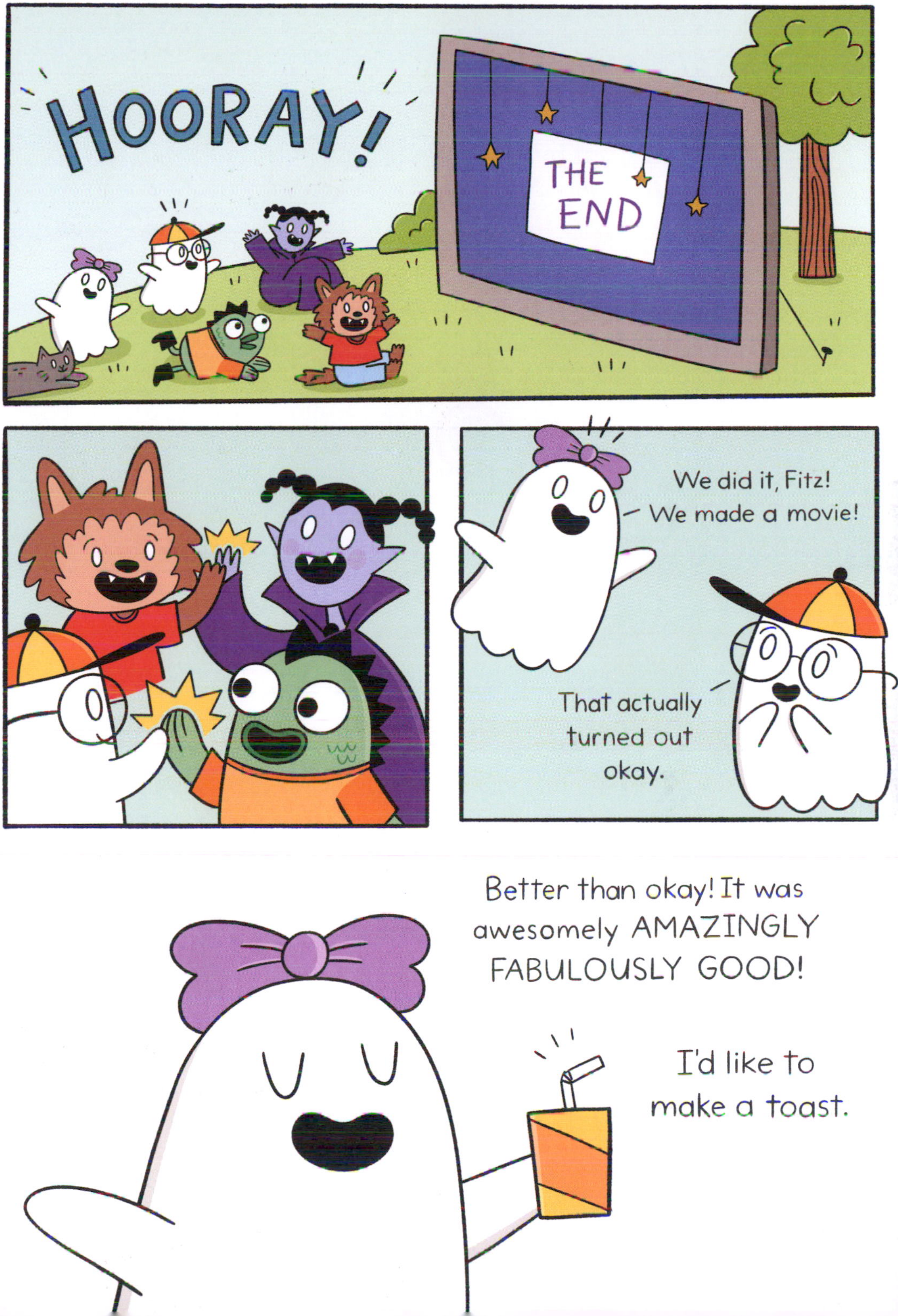
HOORAY!
THE END
We did it, Fitz! We made a movie!
That actually turned out okay.
Better than okay! It was awesomely AMAZINGLY FABULOUSLY GOOD!
I'd like to make a toast.

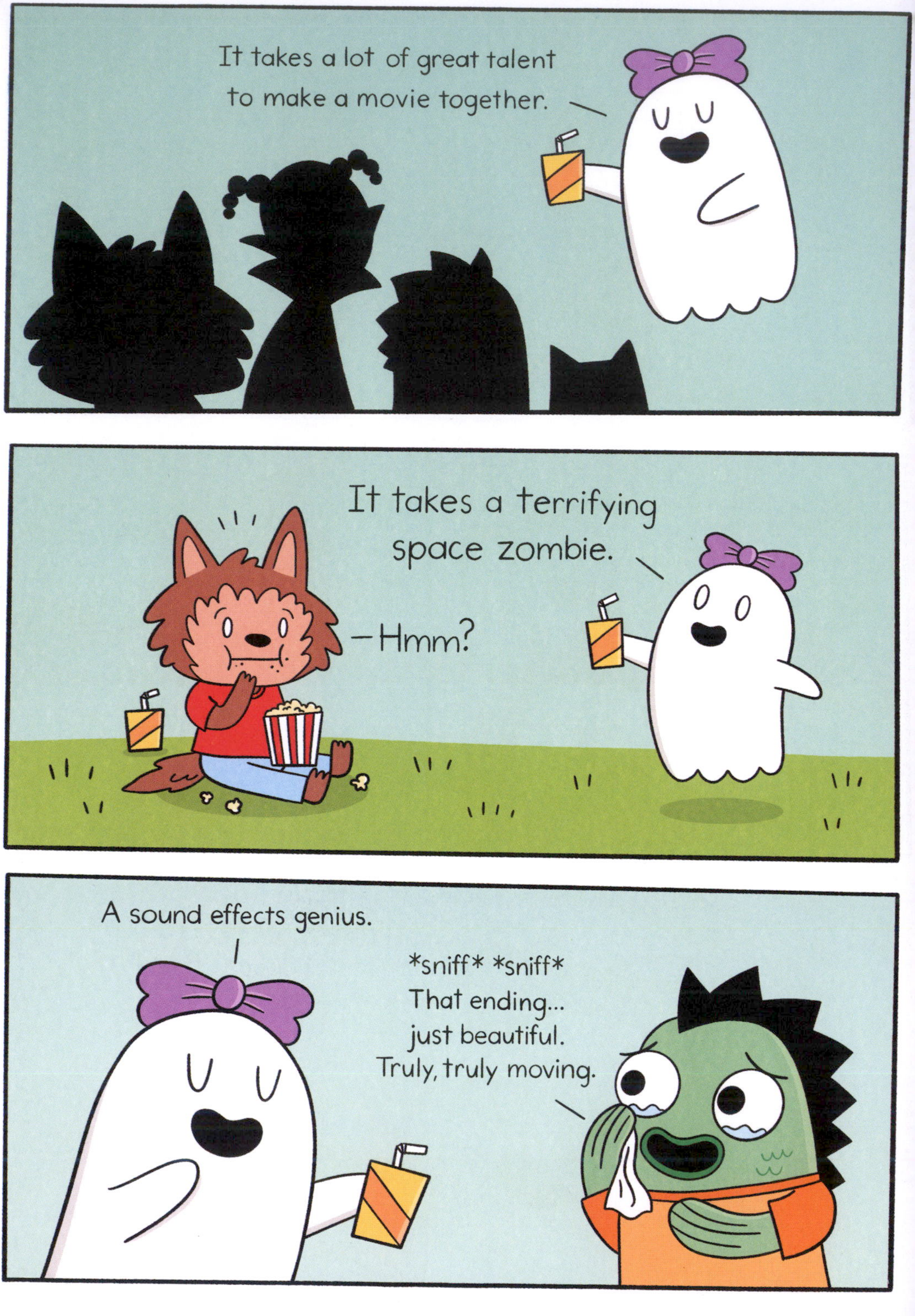
It takes a lot of great talent to make a movie together.
It takes a terrifying space zombie.
—Hmm?
A sound effects genius.
sniff *sniff* That ending... just beautiful. Truly, truly moving.

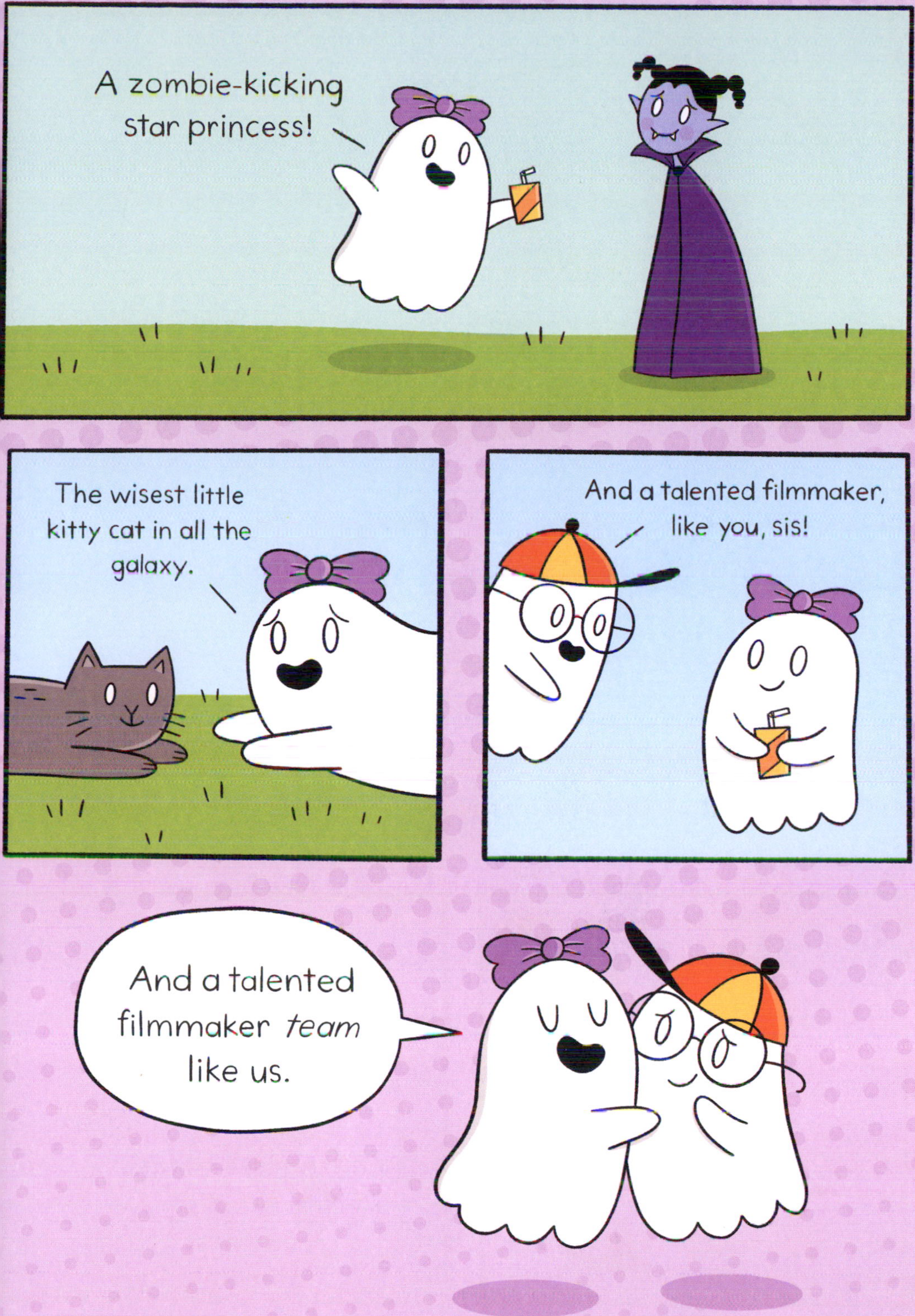
A zombie-kicking star princess!
The wisest little kitty cat in all the galaxy.
And a talented filmmaker, like you, sis!
And a talented filmmaker *team* like us.

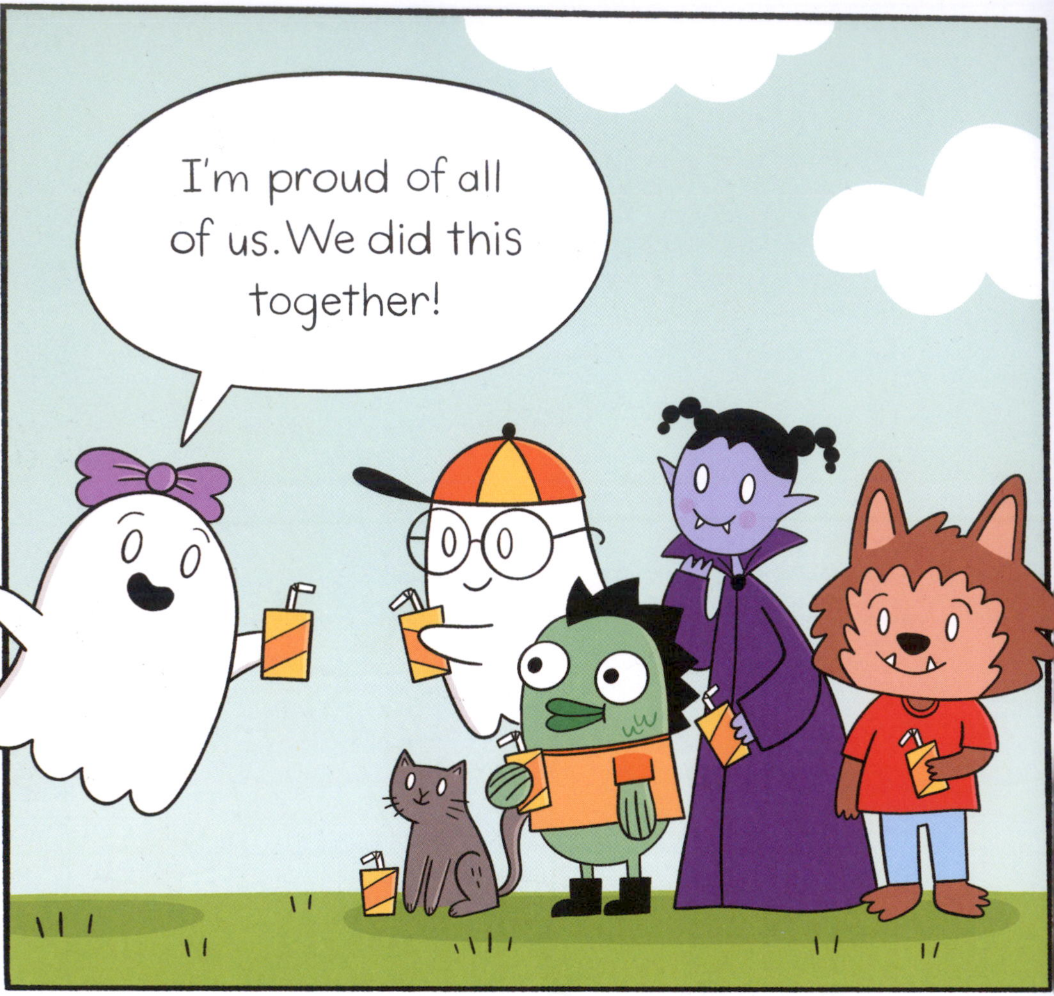
I'm proud of all of us. We did this together!

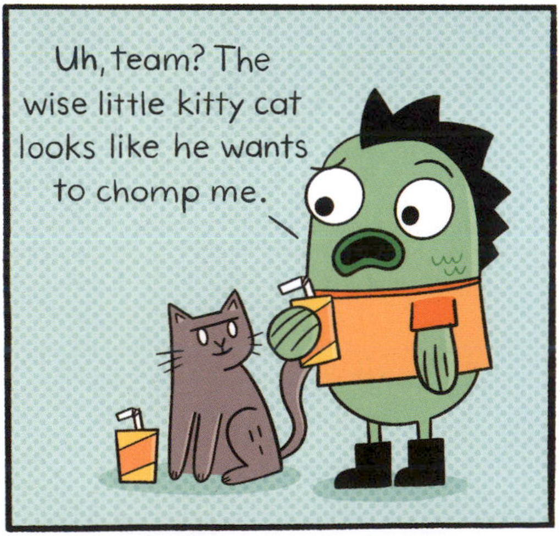
Uh, team? The wise little kitty cat looks like he wants to chomp me.

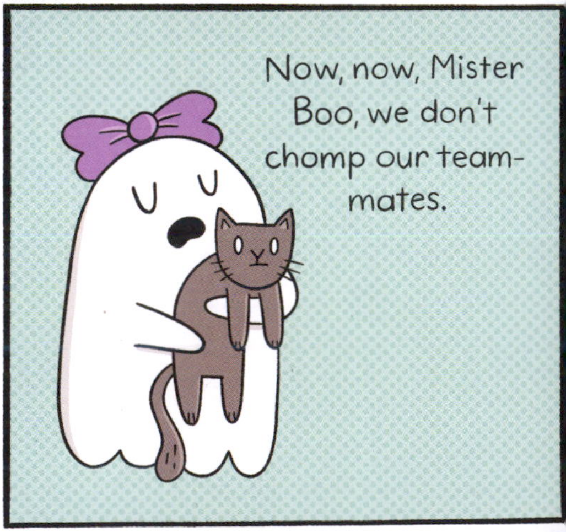
Now, now, Mister Boo, we don't chomp our team-mates.

Cheers, everyone!
We had a beautiful adventure.

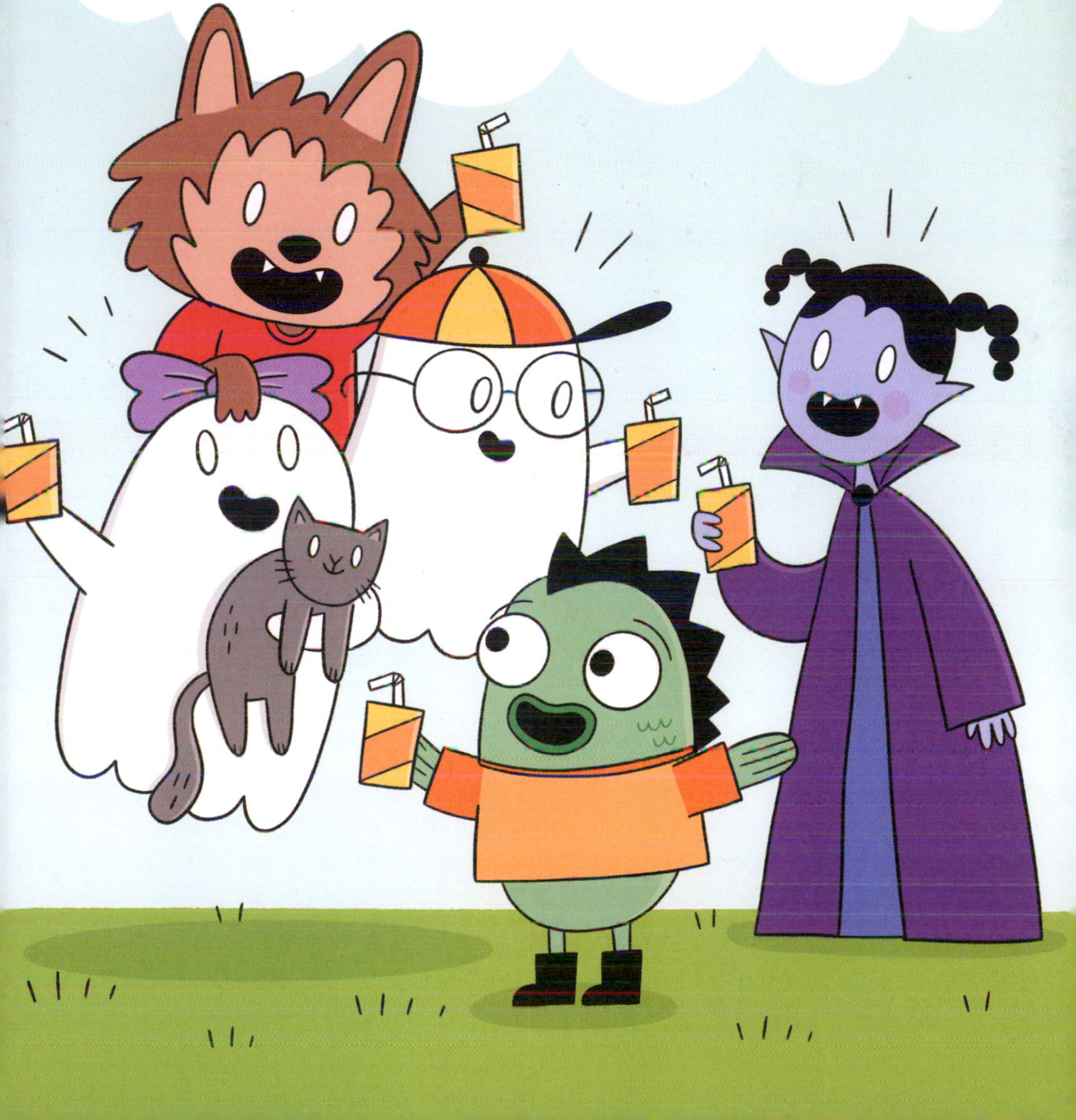

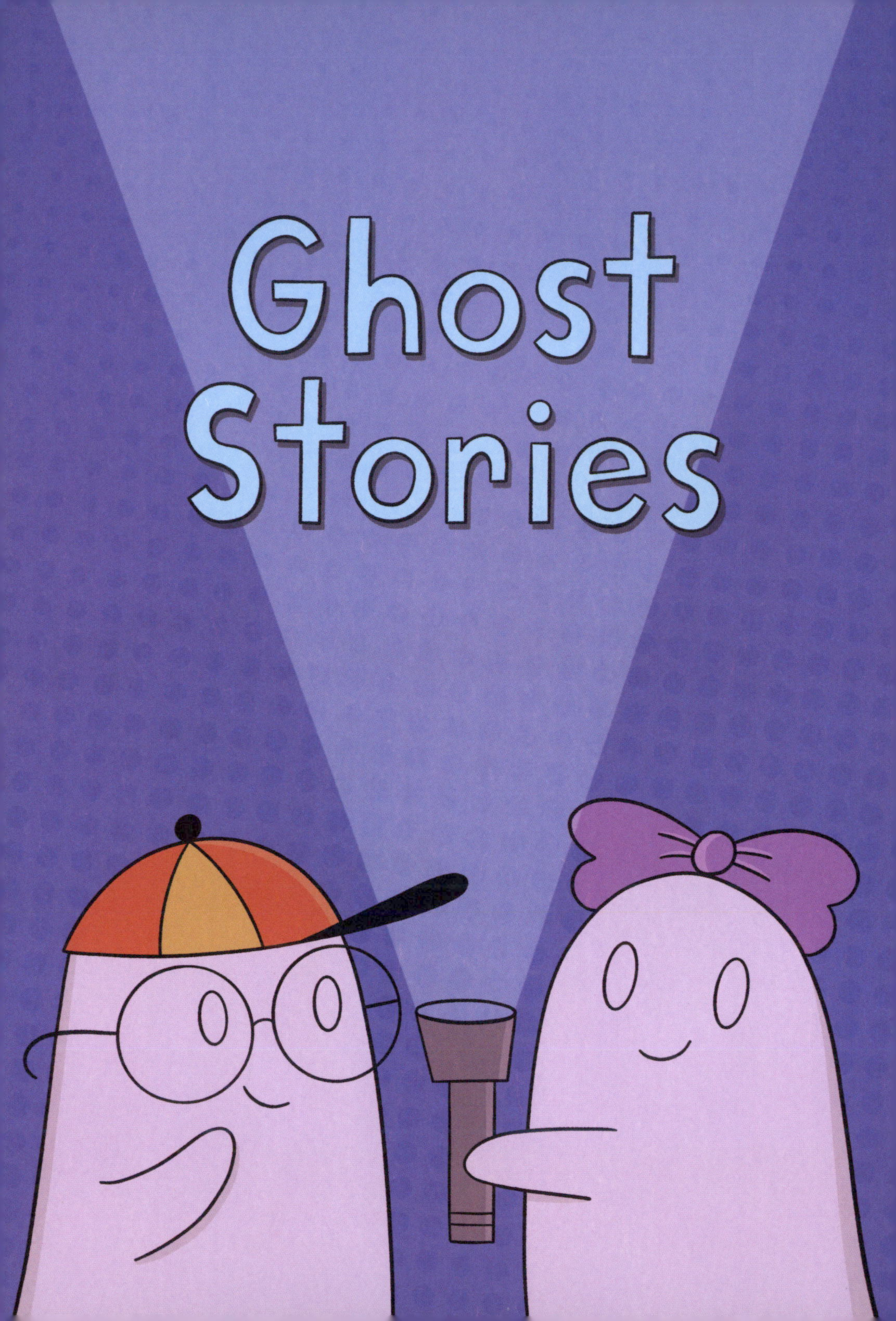
Ghost
Stories

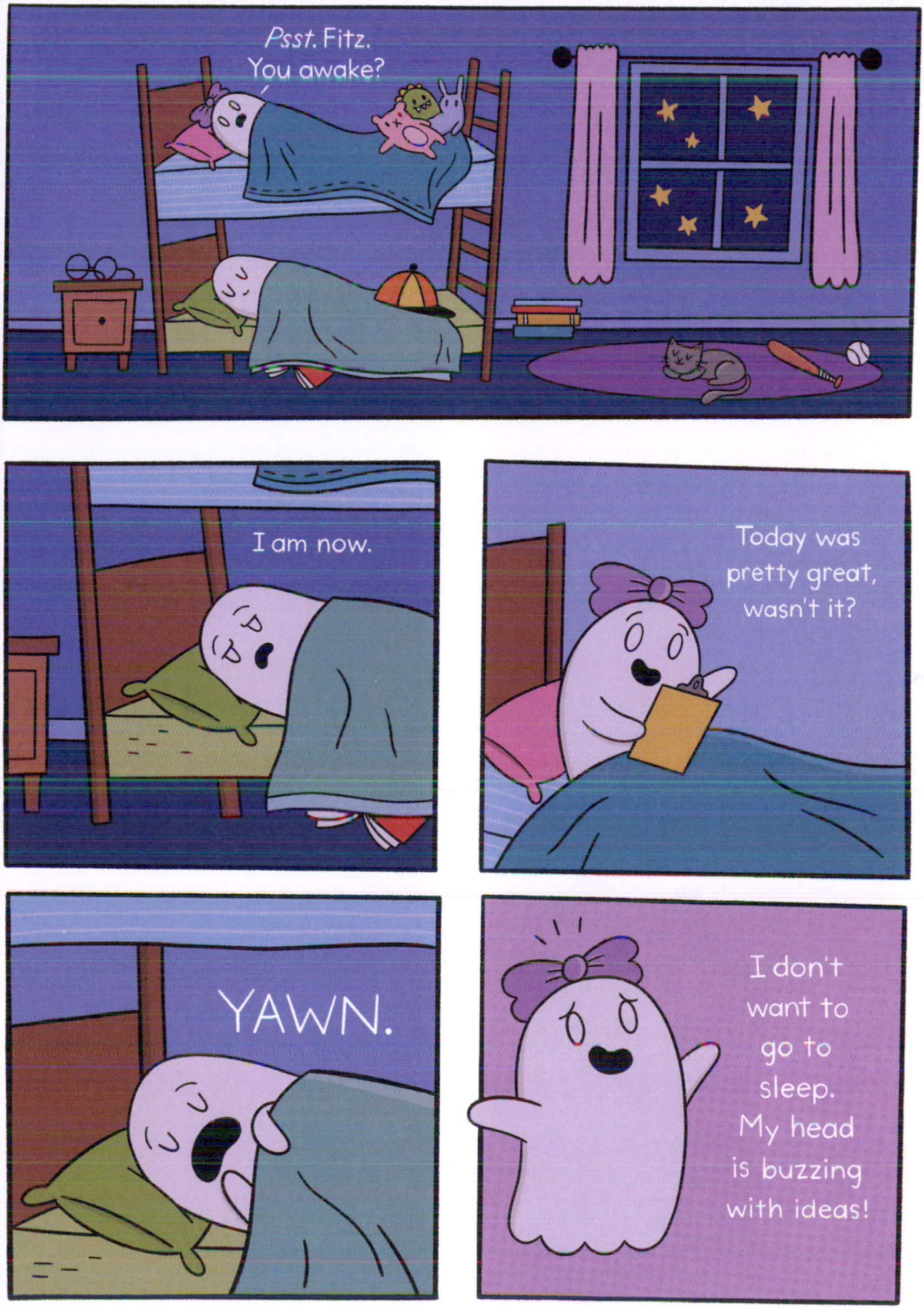
Psst. Fitz. You awake?
I am now.
Today was pretty great, wasn't it?
YAWN.
I don't want to go to sleep. My head is buzzing with ideas!

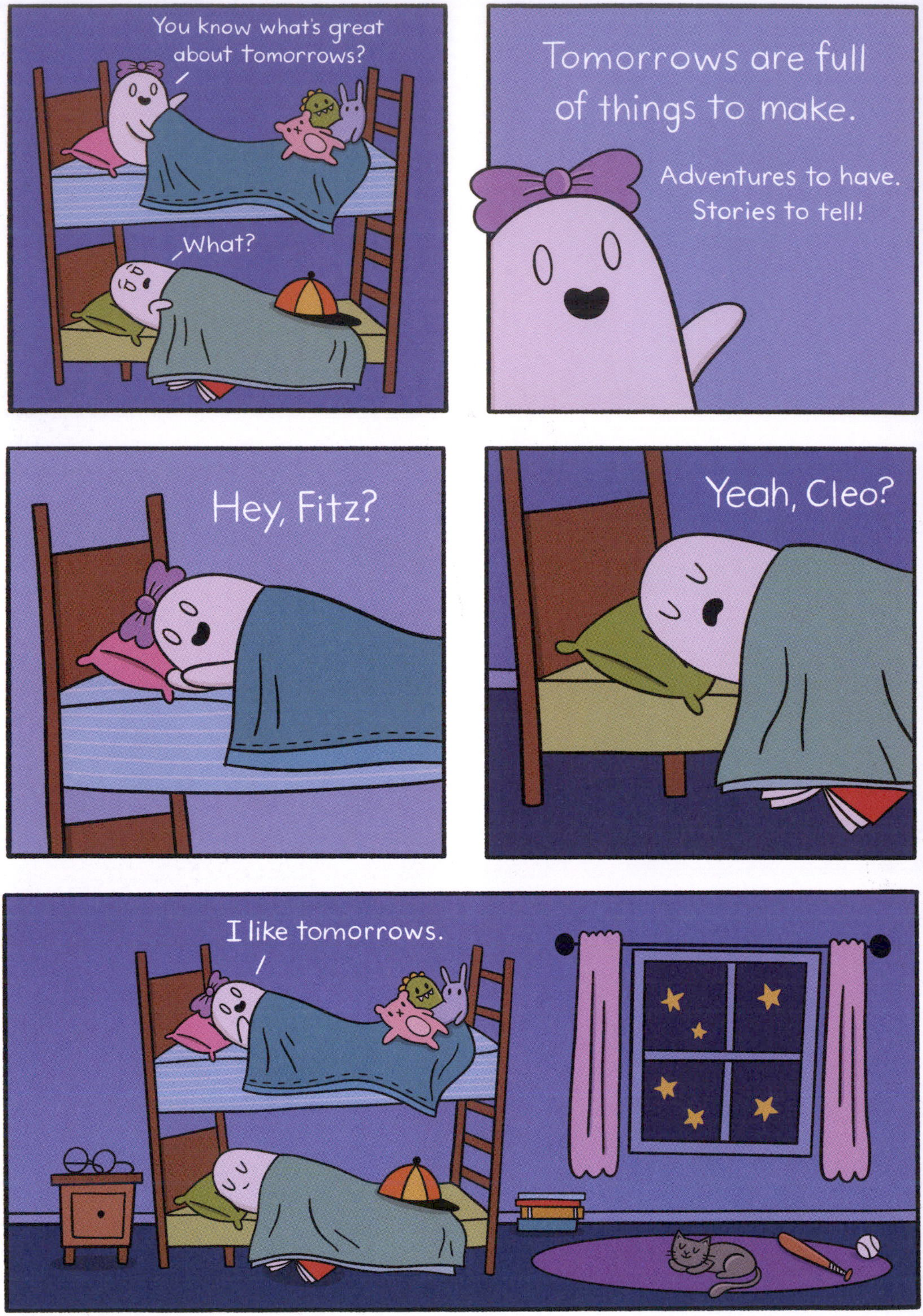
You know what's great about tomorrows?
What?
Tomorrows are full of things to make.
Adventures to have. Stories to tell!
Hey, Fitz?
Yeah, Cleo?
I like tomorrows.

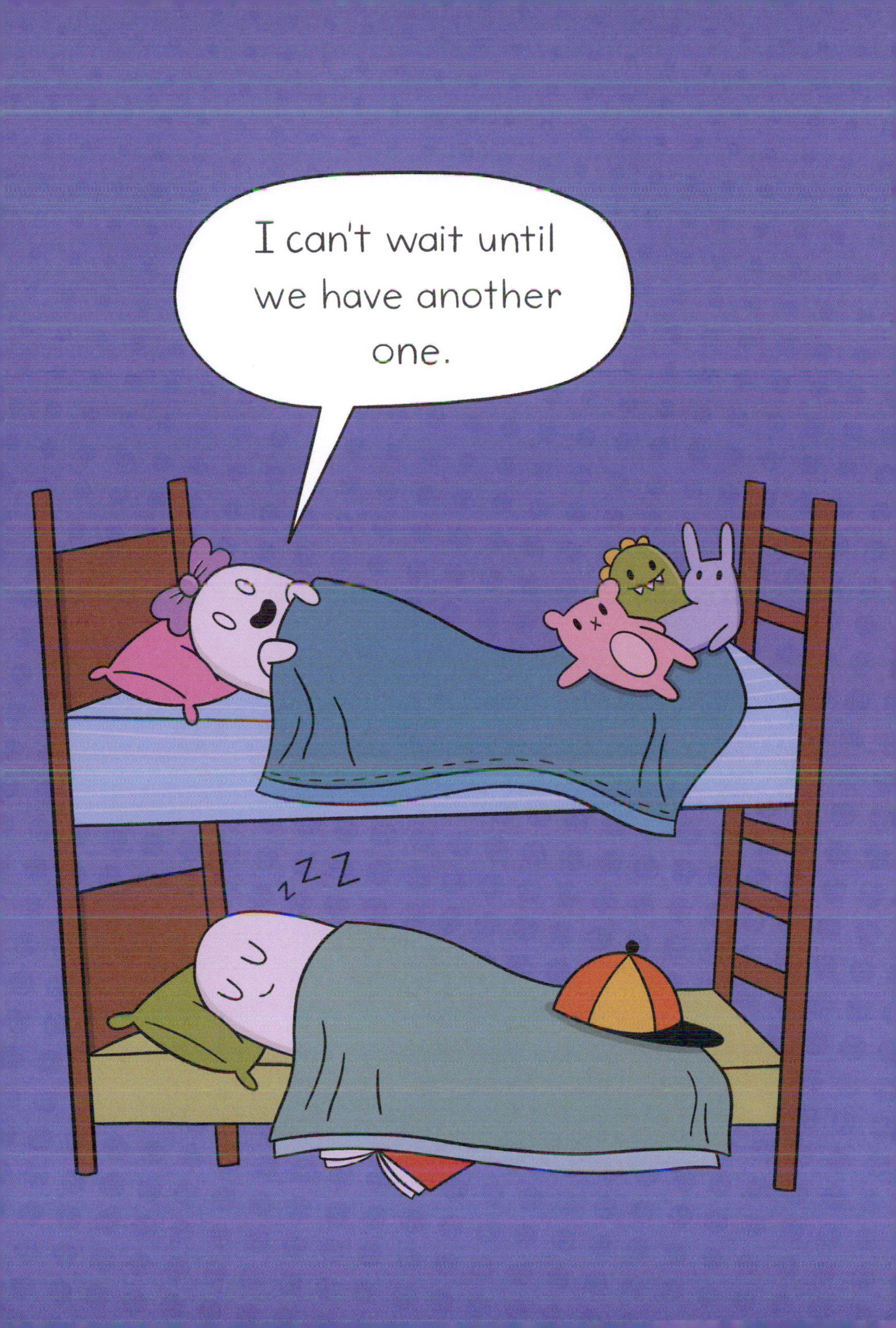
I can't wait until we have another one.
z Z Z